'I'm thinking the standard of culture in the school is improving,' said Dick Wilson, indicating the playground carnage through the window with his cup of whiskey. 'For 'tis the Romans and Britons they're playing at now. When ye first came, Thomas, it was Al Capone every morning . . .'

Ancoats in the 1920s is a wretched industrial slum near Manchester, whose inhabitants, fighting for survival, have no interest in education. But Thomas Davies, a highly qualified young schoolteacher, thinks differently. His runny-nosed, baggy-breeched, violent pupils are going to learn about history, art and the outside world if it's the last thing he does. He will bring the glory that was Greece to the squalor that is Ancoats – not to mention Shakespeare, Verdi, Beowulf, heathenish gods, the American Civil War, and Aeschylus.

Davies's vision, determination and enthusiasm entirely alter his pupils' experience of schooling; but though, through his teaching, relays of youngsters find their way out of the slum to jobs in pleasanter districts, Davies himself is tied to Ancoats by his demanding, widowed mother. Until the onset of war offers him his own chance of escape, and he joins the RAF . . .

Malcolm Lynch, author of *The streets of Ancoats*, himself went to school in that Lancashire ghetto. His warm and funny novel pulses with the life of the now-vanished community, and movingly portrays one man's search for escape and fulfilment.

*Also by Malcolm Lynch*

The streets of Ancoats (1985)

Malcolm Lynch

# They fly forgotten

Constable · London

First published in Great Britain 1987
by Constable and Company Limited
10 Orange Street London WC2H 7EG
Copyright © 1987 by Malcolm Lynch
Set in Linotron Ehrhardt 11pt
and printed in Great Britain by
Redwood Burn Limited,
Trowbridge, Wiltshire

British Library CIP data
Lynch, Malcolm
They fly forgotten
I. Title
823'.914[F]   PR6062.Y5/

ISBN 0 09 467590 2

To every man and woman who stands before a blackboard

# Acknowledgements

The lyrics from 'Penny Lane' on page 180 are reproduced by kind permission of Northern Songs, assigned to Catherine Holmes à Court, © 1967.

The lyrics from 'Yesterday' on page 181 are reproduced by kind permission of Northern Songs, © 1965.

# Foreword

Manchester turned itself into the first industrial city in the world. As a result, it created the first industrial slum in the world – Ancoats. The aim was to pack as many workers as possible into the most meagre dwellings on the smallest amount of ground, surrounded by palatial mills and tall chimneys. Cotton machinery was expensive, people were cheap.

Adding to the overcrowding of these two-up two-down hovels came streams of immigrants from Ireland and Italy.

When the depression came, these human beings were unwanted; they had no value. In order to survive or keep out of the workhouse, many were forced into crime, often violent crime, and a popular saying at the time was – 'If the world needs an enema, they'll do it in Ancoats.'

These unwanted people were only concerned with getting food, clothes and the rent money; education for their children was the last thing they cared about. 'What's the good of learning him to read and write? He'll still end up in Strangeways with the others,' mothers sometimes told the school board inspectors.

On to this scene, in the late 1920s, came a brand new teacher, fresh from college and wet behind the ears.

'They've knocked the head off Jesus.'

But Thomas was too excited, too full of himself, too proud of himself to take in what his mother was saying.

'I don't think you heard a blessed word I said,' she repeated. 'I said they've knocked the head off Jesus.'

'Off Jesus,' said Thomas like a dull, absent-minded echo. He was admiring himself in the mirror; tilting his university mortarboard at a rakish angle.

'And the woman next door has taken in a lodger, a Dutchman or a Pole or something. And I knew you'd like liver and onions on the day of your graduation. In fact it was coming back from the butcher's with the liver through Whitworth Park that I noticed they'd knocked the head off; you couldn't miss it. You know the statue I mean, Thomas; the one where Jesus is surrounded by little children looking up at him, and it says "Suffer little children to come unto Me." Well, they came unto him all right, and it was him they made suffer by knocking his head off. Oh, and there's a packet of cigarettes on the mantelpiece by the clock. It'll be the statue of King Edward next, just you mark my words. Hooligans, that's what they are, and Moss Side used to be such a nice district. Just look at this street; terraced it may be, but they're all Georgian houses; class that once was – '

'The glory that was Greece,' added Thomas.

'Time was when doctors and lawyers lived here, and their ladies were dressed in crinolines, and they danced the waltz, and they rode in carriages with parasols. And I wouldn't eat your food with your new cap and gown on, Thomas; you'll get fried onion down it.'

'It's probably the last time I'll wear it, mom,' said Thomas, 'so I'm making the most of the occasion.'

'Nonsense! When you start teaching in one of those ivy-covered swanky schools like you used to read about in *The Gem* and *The Magnet*, which I bought you every Friday, you'll have to wear your cap and gown all the time, even when you're chasing boys across the playing fields. I remember all the front covers, and that's how you'll be.'

Thomas had been cutting through the tough liver and making it squeak on the plate. He stopped cutting; he'd lost his appetite. How was he going to tell her that of his own free will he wasn't going to teach in a swanky school? Oh yes, he'd been given the opportunity only that very afternoon, and it had been a great afternoon, a wonderful afternoon. The graduation ceremony in the hall of Owens College had been like a cathedral service; the organ had played, and the choir had sung 'Gaudeamus Igitur'. And then the Dean of the Faculty had asked him to return next term as a tutor. His grades for the honours degree had been so high that nothing could prevent him getting an eventual pro-fessorship or doctorate, and all on a fair-sized salary. But he'd already obtained a post. He was going to start as a common schoolmaster at Raglan Street Elementary School in Ancoats. The Dean asked him why.

'I'd like to go where the soil is unbroken and do some planting, sir.'

'I thought your degree was in arts, not agriculture,' said the Dean. 'But have it your way, and the best of luck.'

'And you'll bloody need it,' said Hopkins when he joined his mates in the quadrangle. 'They'll kill you.'

'They'll crucify you,' added Hayward. 'They'll have your guts for bloody garters. They call Raglan Street the Amazon. No man has ever reached its source and returned to tell the tale.'

'They've no money in Ancoats, and therefore no food, and therefore they're hungry,' said Hopkins. 'And you're going as breakfast. They eat teachers. *Quod erat demonstrandum*.'

And now Thomas had to break the news to his mother; that's if she'd give him half a chance; once she started talking, she never knew when to stop.

'Your dad would have been so proud of you,' she said, straightening the mortarboard which he'd tipped to a slant. She looked up at the large framed picture above the mantelpiece of a young officer in the Royal Flying Corps. 'Let's see now, it's 1929 and your dad was shot down in 1917, so that's twelve years ago, and you were only seven at the time; but even on his last leave he said how proud he was of you and what great hopes he had for your future. "He'll grow up to be a good son," he said, "and if anything ever happens to me, he'll always look after you, he'll never leave you." Those were his very last words, and he saluted me, and the train puff-puffed away leaving you holding my hand on the platform, such a tiny hand you had.'

Thomas let his knife and fork drop; he abandoned the liver and onions; he knew what was coming next.

'Your dad once waved to Baron Von Richthofen and the Baron waved right back to him when they were both in their aeroplanes – ' As a small boy, he'd once asked if they'd been shaking their fists at each other because they were vexed. 'Oh, goodness me, no!' she'd replied. 'They were very very friendly. It was just that neither of them had got any more bullets left. But just imagine a famous German baron waving to your father, for barons are almost royalty, and German royalty is connected with our royalty. Mind you, nobody in this street knows your dad was once waved to by a German baron, and I'm not going to tell them even if they ask me.'

For a second, Thomas looked for courage from the clock on the mantelpiece. It was a black marble clock; it was meant to represent a Greek temple with a sloping roof; it even had a brass column on either side of the clock face. Thomas had always pretended he could live inside the clock, and control the works and make it always Christmas Eve. The clock lost ten minutes every week, and had to be adjusted on Saturday nights.

'It's taken all my widow's pension to keep you at university but it's what your dad would have wished, and I know I'll never regret it,' she went on.

'I'm starting work on Monday,' he said. 'As a schoolmaster in an Ancoats school.'

'Ancoats? Ancoats?' Her eyes widened with shock and she slumped in her easy chair.

'Ancoats,' said Thomas. 'It isn't far away. I shall be able to go on my bike and save the tram fare.'

'But you can't go to Ancoats! It's dirty and evil! It's where the workhouse is, and the tramp ward. And there's murders nearly every week. Thomas, you'll be tainted, you'll be tarred with their brush. Just like you've gone and got onion down your new gown in spite of my warning you.'

11

Carolina moon, keep shining,
Shining on the one who waits for me!
Carolina moon, I'm pining,
Pining for the place I long to be.

Thomas Davies's bicycle rattled over the cobbles of Every Street; it rattled even more over the rougher cobbles of Raglan Street. And there was the small black school he was to teach at. It was ugly; it looked as though it had been born in the coal cellar of the workhouse. Perhaps the workhouse was its mother, for the workhouse was a much larger and grander building. And the giant gasometer behind the school was its father. That's how Thomas figured it out. All the windows had wire netting nailed over them; the tops of the high walls had broken glass cemented on them.

He'd been told to report early in order to meet the headmaster before school began. As he leaned his bicycle against the wall and took off his cycle clips he heard the unbelievable but unmistakable strains of a violin coming from inside. The melody was 'Danny Boy'. Well, it was a good sign. Art was not dead in Raglan Street. He followed the music up the corridor, and it led him to the headmaster's office. Inside, a middle-aged man, grey hair, grey suit and red tie, obviously the headmaster, swayed daintily on his feet as he played. When Thomas walked in, he put the violin on the table, removed the handkerchief from under his chin, wiped tears from his eyes with it, blew his nose loudly on it, and held his hand out.

''Tis a wonderful melody is it not? Some call it the Londonderry Air, some just the Derry Air, but Derry Air sounds too much like a French arse, and so, to be perfectly neutral and decent, I call it Danny Boy. I'm Dick Wilson, formerly of Queen's University in the County of Antrim, and currently headmaster of Raglan Street, Ancoats, in the County of old Lucifer. And ye'll be Mr Thomas Davies.'

'That's right.'

'Well, the devil knows how long ye'll be staying – some don't even last a term – but I'll support ye in anything ye have a mind to do, including the building of a gallows in the playground. Sure most of the kids'll be following their fathers' footsteps, so it'll help familiarise them. Ye'll always find a drop o' the hard stuff in

12

me cupboard, which ye'll be needing from time to time. Ah, sure the little buggers stole me painting of Queen Victoria, and the Boyhood of Raleigh, and the General Gordon getting himself killed in Khartoum – but they'd not dare touch me bottle of Irish for fear of the unholy repercussions. And if ye think people will admire ye for coming here, ye'll be sadly mistaken, for the nearest ye'll get to a laurel wreath for teaching here is a lavatory seat slammed over your head like a harness.'

'What do I teach?'

'Ah now, I'm thinking ye should rephrase that question to be asking what ye don't teach. Ye don't teach singing, for there's a Miss Cowgill for that. And ye don't teach the physical jerks and the football, for there's a Mr Macgregor for such things.'

'Four teachers, including yourself?'

'To be precise, three schoolmasters and one schoolmistress, if ye please. And there's over three hundred scholars. The girls' school is next door, and ye'll have noticed the high walls and the broken glass, for 'tis the state of puberty our scholars are entering into, and if it wasn't for the deterrents the little buggers'd be fornicating all over the place, would ye know.'

'It's a hell of a lot of pupils for four.'

'Not "pupils". 'Tis scholars we call the little sods. And things are not too bad, for we treble up, d'y'see? Get to school early, and write up sums on one blackboard, history dates on another, handwriting on another and so on. Then ye stride from classroom to classroom with the strap in your hand. I'll be issuing ye with a strap, but be sure and take it home with ye, for they'll steal it as soon as your back's turned.'

'Hardly the best way to give the scholars an education.'

'Education? And what'd they be wanting with an education? We know it, and they know it. This district is as tough as an old boot. There aren't many jobs going in this part of the world, and any that are will certainly not go to Ancoats boys. Ach, maybe a bit of shovelling here and there; a bit of sweeping up from time to time. Half of them get sent to reformatories before they leave school anyway. We just keep 'em here until they're fourteen cos the law says so; and they get free dinners and they get free milk.'

Mr Macgregor arrived – Charlie Macgregor. He was a big man, with close-cropped red hair and thick bulging muscles; a fit man; a strong man; a well-built man; the man on the porridge packet. He was just a few years older than Davies. When they shook hands, Thomas thought his knuckles were going to turn into powder.

'And here's a hand, my trusty fiere, and gie's a hand o' thine,' he said.

'Like in the song, eh?' said Thomas.

'Song? That's nae a song; that's an anthem, laddie.'

In bobbed Miss Cowgill, a little roly-poly dumpling of a woman, aged about forty. Her face was round, her breasts were round, her stomach was round, her bottom was round, her hands were round, and Thomas had little doubt her legs and arms were round also. Her blonde hair was basin-fringed. She could have been a Socialist.

'Summer is a-coming in,' she tinkled. 'Loud sing ye cuckoo.' He tried to shake her hand but only managed to grip her fingers; her fingers were soft and round and slipped away from his hand. She bounced out of the office tra-la-la-ing Mendelssohn's 'Spring Song'.

Mr Wilson tapped his forehead with his finger. 'Ye'll have gathered we're all a bit tapped, so ye will. But whether 'twas because we were tapped in the first place that we came here, or whether being here has made us tapped, ye'll be finding out for yourself, so you will.' He popped his head out through the door, pulled a whistle from his waistcoat pocket and blew it with Cup Final loudness. 'We used to have a handbell,' he said; 'but it went like everything else. This whistle was the one used to send the Flying Scotsman on its first ever journey along the tracks, or so the boy told me who sold it to me; but if ye ask me I think it's a blooming old police whistle.'

There was a sudden stampede through the corridor; it sounded more like three thousand boys thumping, banging, hitting, slapping and kicking than three hundred.

'Are ye sure no ye'd not be wanting a wee gargle of the hard stuff before ye face them?'

'No, thank you.'

'Then don't forget your strap, for ye're about to enter the cages of lions.'

'Aye,' added Mr Macgregor. 'Welcome to your gory bed or to victorie.'

There was something of a massacre taking place in the first

classroom; arms and legs were twisting and twirling in all directions. Thomas banged his strap on the desk like a thundercrack. There was immediate silence; but it was an unnerving silence, not even a cough or a boot shuffle. He knew he was being scrutinised. He looked from face to face, then his eyes took in the room itself. On the blackboard, somebody had chalked a crude drawing of a backside. There was a radiation of tittering as he looked at it.

He lifted up his desk lid, and it was as though somebody had thumped him in the stomach, for the desk had been filled with stinking horse muck. Once more there were waves of tittering. His instinct was to lash out at everybody but he controlled himself. No, that wasn't the way; but what was the way?

'Who's the best fighter? The cock o' the class?' he asked with a friendly sort of smile. Most of the class turned to look at one particular boy. The boy gripped his hands in a winner's clench. 'I am, sir.'

'Name?'

'Cathcart, sir.'

'Come here then, Cathcart; let's all have a look at you.'

The boy swaggered out to the front of the class.

'You look like a clever boy, Cathcart,' said Mr Davies. 'Tell me, tell all of us, what you know about Steve Donoghue?'

'He's a famous jockey, sir. And he's won the Derby a lot of times.'

'He must be very rich?'

'Yes, sir.'

'Would you like to be a rich and famous jockey like Steve Donoghue?'

'Yes, sir.'

'Easy! That's what I'm here for; to help you become rich and famous,' continued Mr Davies. 'Now, Cathcart, a jockey has to start at the bottom. He begins as a stable boy, cleaning out the stables and brushing the horses down, doesn't he?'

'I suppose so, sir.'

'No "suppose" about it! So then I want you to start your career by getting a brush and dustpan, a rag and some soap, and cleaning out my desk. Some day, when you've won the Grand National, you'll thank me.'

'But I didn't do it.'

15

'I'm sure you didn't. It was a horse or several horses, but I don't see any of them in the classroom. Get on with it, or I'll give you another lesson in horse-racing; how to whip an animal's hindquarters in order to make it jump fences.'

'But it wasn't me! It wasn't me!'

'I don't know who it was. I shall leave you to thank him personally for helping you get started on a promising career. You can thank him in the playground.'

'I'll bloody smash your face in!' Cathcart shouted to one of the boys in the back of the class. 'I'll bleeding pulverise you!' Cathcart went out to collect the cleaning tackle, and Thomas was well content in his own mind that rough justice would prevent any more horse muck being packed into his desk. He now turned to the blackboard, and examined the crude drawing as though inspecting a masterpiece.

'And I see somebody else wants to start at the bottom,' he smiled. Then he became stern: 'Hold your hands out, palms upwards!' he said. He picked the boy with chalk on his fingers, and led him out to the front.

'Name?'

'Alker, sir.'

'And you're the artist responsible for this posterior, are you?'

'I don't know, sir.'

'A posterior is a bottom or backside.'

'Yes, sir.'

'I don't suppose you can spell bottom, posterior or backside?'

'No, sir.'

'No, of course not. To you it would be a bum. Would the class tell Alker how to spell "bum"?'

'B-U-M!' was shouted out.

'A lot of artists became famous by painting and sculpting bums,' he went on. 'There was Michelangelo, Leonardo da Vinci, Botticelli, Titian. I don't suppose any of you know those names. In all probability most of you don't even know your own names. I suppose you too, Alker, would like to become rich and famous? As an artist?'

'No, sir. Please, sir; no, sir.'

'Oh, but you have a gift, Alker. You belong to the world.'

'Yes, sir.'

'Tell me, has one of the boys posed for you as your model? Did

16

he take his trousers down and bend over while you drew him?'

'No, sir.'

'Ah, then it's a self portrait.'

'I don't know what you mean.'

'It's your own bum. Somebody held a mirror for you, perhaps?'

'No, sir. It's nobody's bum. It's just a bum.'

'Come now, there's no such person as a nobody. It can't be just a bum, like the smile of the Cheshire cat was just a smile. It must be your own bum.'

'Yes, sir.'

'Very good. Well then, Alker, all good artists give their pictures a title, and they sign it. So I want you to take this piece of chalk and write "My Bum" on the left of your drawing, and sign it on the bottom right. The class have already taught you how to spell bum, haven't they? Alas, there's always a snag; artists nearly always have to suffer for their art; and I do hope that at playtime none of the class try to take your trousers down in order to make sure you have created a perfect reproduction of yourself.'

Cathcart returned to the classroom with a bucket and shovel.

'I take back what I said about there being no such person as a nobody,' said Mr Davies; 'for here we have one. Stand where you are for a second, Cathcart, will you? Now, boys, thousands of years ago when there was no reading or writing, people were very primitive. Cathcart here is an excellent example of early boy. What these primitive people began to do was paint pictures of hunting scenes on the walls of their caves. Alker has demonstrated how crude and simple these first paintings were ...' And Mr Davies began a lesson on the Stone Age. No boy dared fart or belch or plop his finger in his mouth; they were scared of being ridiculed before the class.

The police whistle blew for playtime. Alker stayed behind.

'Please, sir, can I stay in the classroom? Only you've put a notion in their heads, and they'll be waiting outside to pull me trousers down.'

'I'm sorry; I didn't mean to give them notions. Of course you can stay in the sanctuary of the classroom. But I'll give you a chance to exercise your free will, which all men are born with. Your beautiful drawing can stay on the blackboard all day for the other classes to admire, or you can spend playtime cleaning the

17

board and then filling it with specimens of your best roundhand writing.'

'I'll clean the board and do the writing, sir.'

'An excellent choice!' Thomas chalked up 'Michelangelo, Leonardo da Vinci, Botticelli and Tintoretto.'

'Good Italian names,' he smiled. 'Copy them over and over again.'

Thomas left the classroom, leaving Alker to mutter under his breath that he'd kill the first Italian kid what came within spitting distance of him.

The day passed with lesson after lesson in classroom after classroom, and all went well. There were occasional touches of the circus, as when a boy, who made a cockadoodle-doo noise, was invited, with aggressive encouragement from the class, to stand on his desk and go through the range of farmyard noises from Rover the friendly sheepdog to Buttercup the contented cow.

There were more primitive acts. It seemed to Thomas that the most popular trick of all the classes was for a boy to break wind as loudly as he could, with the rest of the boys holding their noses. It was only the action of the nose-holding which told Thomas what had taken place, for there was so much noise going on outside, the grinding and ting-ting of tram cars, the rumbling carts and clopping of horses, the sudden puffing of locomotives and clanking of shunted wagons, that the small explosion from a boy's bowels had no chance of being heard; there were also so many odours from the mills, sulphur, coke, rubber and pear drops, that a whiff of stomach gas could not compete.

Thomas ordered the boy to stand on his desk and continue breaking wind until it could be heard over the tram cars.

'Yeh, do what sir says!' the rest of the class shouted. 'You could become a world famous farter!'

'Please, sir . . .' whimpered the boy.

'Yes? What is it?'

'Please, sir. If I don't stop, I'll kaki in me keks.'

'Off to the lavatory then! Quick as you can!'

There were other noises; singing noises from the hall; and throughout the day the singing never stopped. He peeped into the hall once or twice, and there was round little Miss Cowgill standing at the piano, playing it with one hand, conducting by a knitting needle with the other. Fifty boys stood in mesmerised obedience, and they sang:

This is the weather the cuckoo likes,
    And so do I;
When showers betumble the chestnut spikes,
    And nestlings fly.

He wondered what magic or magnetism Miss Cowgill waved from her knitting needle. Her songs were cissie songs, full of daisies and cuckoos, yet the boys sang them, and not one boy put a cuckoo out of place.

Maybe it was her attempt to bring springtime to Ancoats, to create the impossible.

He could hear Macgregor's loud voice from the playground. Macgregor didn't give his classes Swedish drill or physical jerks; he marched them smartly around the playground to 'erf-arf, erf-arf, erf-arf! Pick 'em up there! Erf-arf!'

Occasionally, and when least expected, Mr Wilson's violin played 'Danny Boy'.

At home time the four teachers were too tired to talk; they nodded to each other and went their ways, leaving the caretaker to clean the blackboards, empty the baskets and brush the floors.

Thomas walked out of the school pleased with himself. He had pitted his wits against the boys, and he had won. It was a district of violence, the kids were violent; he was determined never to use the violence of the leather strap; he could lash them with his tongue, divide them, turn one boy against another. Sarcasm would be his weapon. Sarcasm was a strange language they couldn't understand, and therefore feared. He was a druid and had the power of words over his tribe.

His bicycle had been stolen. He had to go home on the tram.

# Full well they laughed

'Ah well, ye're fitting in nicely, me fine feller.'

'Thank you.'

Mr Wilson poured himself out a drop of the hard stuff, and indicated a chair for Thomas to sit on.

'But ye must always remember never to become one of them, never get yourself involved, never go round to their houses, keep aloof, aye, keep well aloof. For 'tis their respect ye'll be losing if ye don't, and that's a fact, so it is. This is a ghetto; a ghetto, me boy, that's what it is. Irish and Italians and a few English and Germans, and none of them knowing who the hell they are or where they are or what the blooming heck they're doing here. Sure even the English think they're immigrants. They live in squalor and bloody misery. Their conditions are worse than anything the great and mighty Charles Dickens wrote about sixty years ago, and that's a fact. They steal from the rich in order to keep out of the workhouse, and can ye blame 'em? They have to steal to pay the doctor's bills, and there's many a bill comes their way in that line of country with the croup, meningitis, scarlet fever, consumption, venereal disease and maybe a wee touch of smallpox thrown in for good measure. Still, they've got priests and nuns to send their souls all nice and neatly washed and ironed to heaven. Sure sometimes they even have to steal to die. There was a couple of young lads, brothers they were, sent to the reformatory just before you came. Their dad had died, and they'd beaten up a prostitute in a back entry to get her night's takings in order to pay for their dad's funeral. They told the magistrate in the children's court that it was better than having their dad put in a pauper's grave in Queens Park. There y'are now; what d'ye make of that, eh? Course, the little sods have got us; and all we can do is keep 'em in warm rooms with a roof above 'em till the law says they can sign on at the Labour Exchange. Sure if we can give 'em a bit of education while they're here, all

20

well and good. Though 'tis often in my mind I'm thinking our main function is to distribute free milk.' He took a swig of whiskey from his teacup, then smiled to change the subject.

'Tell me, Thomas, me fine young feller me lad, have ye a sideline?'

'A what?'

'Ach, sure ye know what a sideline is. No self-respecting schoolmaster should be without one.' He rubbed his forefinger in the palm of his other hand. ''Tis a bit of the ready, the spondulics, the money ye pick up on the side. Ah, but then ye're not married, I forgot; for if ye were married and had to live on a schoolmaster's paltry pay, ye'd be taking up lodgings in one of those pigsties our dear little scholars live in, and that'd never do, would it now? For 'tis aloof and away from it all ye must be. Tell me, me bold rapparee, are ye otherwise engaged this Saturday evening?'

Thomas took it like a royal command and said he wasn't.

'Then I'll be inviting ye to be my guest at the Bradford Road Pit Workingman's Club. The 53 tram drops ye off at the door, and be there at seven of the clock sharp.'

'I will.'

Thomas hoped there would be chance to ask Mr Wilson about the secret of Miss Cowgill's magic spell, but there wasn't. All in a jiffy Mr Wilson blew the whistle, and there was the morning stampede. The little round lady herself poked her head round the door.

'The lark's on the wing, the snail's on the thorn!' she rippled; then she tra-la-la-ed Schubert's Serenade as she bounced down the corridor.

Mr Macgregor's head came next: 'The trumpets sound, the banners fly, the glittering spears are ready; the shouts of war are heard afar, the battle closes thick and bloody!'

Just a few minutes later the hall was singing:

As I was going to Strawberry Fair,
   Singing, singing buttercups and daisies,
I met a maiden taking her wares, fol-de-dee.
   Her eyes were blue, and golden her hair
As she went on to Strawberry Fair.

21

Thomas had his head bent over a bowl containing vinegar and water, and his mother was combing through his hair with a special fine-tooth comb, known as a louse trap. She had already scolded Thomas for using the term; it was vulgar, and was not a laughing matter.

'Three whole years at Manchester University just to get lice in your hair,' she said, as two more of the creatures dropped into the water and began swimming for their lives.

'It can't be helped. Sometimes I have to bend my head near theirs to correct their work.'

'And there are flea bites on your neck. I hope you don't bring them home with you.'

'No, mom. They get off at Pin Mill Brow; they don't like leaving Ancoats; it's where they belong.'

'And it's a pity those foreigners in Ancoats didn't stay where they belonged.'

Thomas laughed: 'Mr Wilson says the fleas that get on us are lucky; they get a taste of education before they die.'

'And no doubt it'll be parasites and vermin you're going to discuss with him tonight.'

'I don't know, mom. He just asked me to meet him at seven o'clock.'

'You'd have been better staying in and soaking your head in paraffin to get rid of any nits, but go if you must. I suppose I shall have to get used to being lonely.'

Dick Wilson was waiting outside the workingman's club. At the back of the building the big wheel was turning, and one or two black-faced miners were spitting, as though spitting their lungs up, into the gutter. Dick took Thomas into the very barn of a place. Bare electric lamps hung by their wires from the girders of the roof; the concrete floor was thick with sawdust; all around the sides of the hall were long plain wooden tables and forms; in the body of the hall were upturned tea-chests surrounded by folding wooden chairs. There must have been more than a hundred colliers and their women on the chairs and forms, many of the men's faces were still jet black with coal dust. They all wore caps, and they all had spotless white silk scarves around their necks, for it was after all Saturday night. The men were noisy with laughter and coughing and occasional spitting into spittoons. At the far end of the hall was a stage, or, more accu-

22

rately, a platform with a curtain which opened and closed.

On one side of the hall was a very long bar with three or four bartenders telling thirsty miners to wait their sweat.

'Two pints o' porter, eh, Fred?' Dick asked one of the bartenders.

'Sure, Paddy. Two pints it is.'

'Now I'll be off and leaving ye in a wee while,' Dick told Thomas. 'I'll not be all that long, and Fred here'll be your Gungha Din to prevent ye dying of thirst. All I ask is ye watch out for me cue; sure that's not much to be asking now, is it? Me cue, eh?' He nudged Thomas with his elbow, picked up his small case and sneaked away.

There was an ear-cracking splatter-tatter of a football rattle to get attention. There was a shout for silence, and lights lit up in the biscuit tins on the stage. The curtain opened.

A fat man came on stage. He was dressed as a Bavarian; tight short trousers, wide colourful braces joined by a wider ornate strap back and front, and a William Tell hat with a feather in it on his head. He sang, but not in English; he had no need to sing in English for the audience was with him from the start. It was a song about a '*grosse frau*' and his actions made it perfectly clear what a '*grosse frau*' was. It was a German stein-swaying song, an oompah-pah song. In between his flourishes to indicate big round things back and front, he also slapped himself on his backside, knees and face in the manner of Bavarian slap-dancing, except that he pretended some of his slaps sent him staggering across the stage. The audience joined him in their nearest equivalent to his last song:


Don't put your muck in our dustbin,
  Our dustbin, our dustbin.
Don't put your muck in our dustbin,
  Our dustbin's full.


His act finished, and he went around the club collecting money in his hat.

After the football rattle for quiet, a violin played 'Come Back, Paddy Reilly', and there was wild applause even before the curtain opened and Dick walked on to the stage.

Thomas's porter went down the wrong way and he spluttered, for his headmaster was dressed presumably as a leprechaun; green velvet knee-high knickerbockers, golden stockings, silver buckles on his shoes, a green velvet waistcoat with a golden shamrock embroidered on it, and a green stovepipe hat.

'Good old Paddy!' people shouted. 'Up the Irish! Top of the Morning!'

Dick's dance was a sort of dainty foot shuffle, almost a fairy dance. He stopped and, with an exaggerated Irish accent, told the crowd about an old hen which had followed him home from Shudehill Market. 'Ye'll be thinking to yer good selves that poor ould Paddy Reilly had slipped the blooming bird into his carrier bag when the feller wasn't looking, ah don't I know that's what ye'll be thinking. But 'tis wrong ye'll be, aw indeed it is. Me? Would I be doing such a wicked thing? That rooster followed me every inch o' the way home, so it did. It just winked at me all knowing like when I turned to tell it to go back to the market where it had a good home. Sure it even got on the blessed tram with me and paid its own fare. 'Twas obviously a fully paid-up Christian bird and wanted nothing better than to fill the belly of a poor starving man. Ar, but Holy Mary, Mother of God, wasn't it as hard as a lump o' lead? Did I not have to stuff it with a stick o' dynamite in order to cut it up?' He then sang a song:

Sure that hen was born when they built the Tower of Babel,
    Was fed by Cain and Abel, and lived in Noah's stable,
Nor a shot from the field of Waterloo
    Could not penetrate or devastate
That iron-breasted double-chested solid-crested
    Cockadoodle-dooooooo!

He cajoled the crowd to sing it with him. Then he told a few more stories and sang a few more ditties. Finally he adjusted his violin under his chin, and there was a silence. But before playing he flung his stovepipe hat at Thomas.

'Here y'are now, Mick! Cop for this!'

Thomas caught the hat and leaned against the bar as Dick began to play 'Danny Boy'.

'Hey, Mick!' said the bartender. 'Wake up! He wants you to go round with the hat. That's your cue.'

Thomas shyly shuffled from table to table, and the people, many of whom were weeping at the melody, tossed pennies into the hat.

A woman's voice from the darkness shouted: 'Hey, Mick! Me friend here fancies you. She wants to know if you'll meet her back of the lamp room.'

'Shurrup!' shouted another woman's voice.

Thomas felt his face burning at the idea a girl fancied him, but he hadn't the courage to look and see who it was.

An ordinary and respectable Dick Wilson joined him at the bar and began making shilling columns of the pennies.

'Not a bad night! Not a bad night at all!' said Dick, pushing two of the columns to Thomas. He studied Thomas's face. 'Tell me now, is it surprised ye are at seeing your headmaster make a bloody fool of himself for pennies?'

'A bit.'

'Oh, a bit! Well, how the hell d'y'think I could afford to be a headmaster without earning a few bob on the side, tell me that? I could make this nonsense me full-time occupation and do the music halls, for don't I have 'em eating out of me hand. But somebody's got to keep those little sods at school till they're fourteen, for if there was nobody they'd be going down this very coalmine at five. Think of that, me fine-feathered young friend; five years of age, and their mammies with them.'

Thomas was more interested in the audience; he tried to pick out the girl who fancied him; it was a thrill being fancied; but nobody looked in his direction.

As he and Dick waited for their tram he watched the crowds coming out of the club. The women, young and old, put their shawls over their heads and clutched them. It was only possible to guess at their ages by the shapes of their legs. No white face looked towards him. The crowds laughed and coughed as they turned corners or disappeared down the road. There was a moon between the spokes of the pit cage wheel, and the blue sparks and large round headlight of the tram came towards them.

'Did you have a nice time?' asked his mother, ladling some steaming stew on his plate. 'I know you said not to wait up, but I never rest till I know you're safe at home.'

'It was very interesting.'

'Was it? What did you talk about?'

25

'Money mainly.'

'Thomas! Schoolmasters shouldn't talk about money. It isn't nice.'

One of the boys told Thomas where he'd seen a bicycle just like the one which had been stolen. It was in a second-hand shop in Great Ancoats Street, and Thomas was delighted to see it; he couldn't have been more delighted had he been Alexander the Great being nosed by Bucephalus after it had been missing for a year.

'That's my bike,' he told the woman.

'Good,' she said. 'I like doing business with a person what's decisive. Ten bob and it's yours.'

'What d'y'mean, ten bob? That bike's mine; it was stolen; I recognise it.'

'Aye, but does it recognise you? It isn't making any move in your direction, is it?'

'I think I'd better go to the police.'

'Happen that's the best thing you can do, mister. Tell 'em Honest Amy sent you, cos that's the name they know me by. And as long as you can tell 'em the registration number what's on the frame, I'll be glad to give it you without any charge for storage.'

'I don't know it. I didn't even know there was one.'

'Then that's a bit difficult, isn't it? For the bobbies might think you was trying to cheat Honest Amy by pretending it was yours.'

'Ten bob's a lot of money.'

'Tell you what, call it seven and six, even if I go bankrupt. Y'know what? I think the bike likes you. Look, it's turning its wheel towards you.' She turned the handlebars in his direction with one hand, and held out her other for the money. 'And if ever you want a gramophone, a houseful of furniture or a pair of boots, come to Honest Amy, the Live Wire, for the best bargains in town.'

Thomas was glad to get his bike back. He'd been invited by Charlie Macgregor to join him in the Riverside Hotel just over the Mersey on Saturday night. Cheshire was posh; it was said that people from Manchester had to wipe their feet before crossing any of the bridges into Cheshire; the Riverside Hotel was in Northenden and a long tram ride from Moss Side; on his bike the journey would be free and healthy.

When he arrived his colleague was talking to a sturdily built man at the bar. A pint of beer was pushed over to Thomas with just a nodded greeting and a wag of the finger to keep quiet awhile. The conversation between the two men continued.

'Are you quite sure it's your turn to win?' asked Charlie's companion.

'Ach man, are ye getting punchie or somewhat? Did you not throw me over the ropes at the Assembly Hall in Cheetham Hill just two weeks ago? And me being carried off on a stretcher for pretending to have broken my back? Where's your memory, laddie?'

'I wasn't accusing. I was only asking,' said his companion, quite timidly considering his heavy build.

'So I get my first fall on you in the fifth round. And you foul me a couple of times to get them on my side, is that all right, laddie? You can elbow the ref when he catches you fouling, okay? Then when I'm doubled up in pain, I jump in and get my second fall on you. Then we reverse the routine next week at the Ardwick Stadium.'

Having settled matters, Charlie Macgregor brought Thomas into the conversation. 'All-in-wrestlers,' he explained.

'Your sideline,' said Thomas.

'Aye.'

'Of which no schoolmaster can afford to be without.'

'More than that, Thomas laddie, he'd be in the bloody workhouse without one. Now Jimmy here is Genghis Khan, d'y'see. And me, I fight under the name of Rob Roy, and tonight's bout is in the Northenden Boathouse Stadium at the back of this beerhouse in half an hour, and here's your free ticket; I normally sell 'em. Course we have to do a wee bit rehearsal beforehand for you'd not be wanting downright random paganism to come creeping in with somebody getting hurt, would you now? And fifteen shillings a fight is not to be sneezed at.'

'Are you a schoolmaster?' Thomas asked Genghis.

'In a way, I suppose. I'm a Methodist lay preacher, though I do a bit of bricklaying when there's work available. And this wrestling keeps me from sinning, for there's many a time I'd be tempted to dip into the plate collection on Sunday.'

Charlie put his arm around his opponent's shoulder. 'He tells his flock to turn the other cheek on Sunday, but if he turned the other cheek on Saturday he'd end up with his neck twisted, his knees in a knot, and banging on the canvas for a submission. Fifteen bob, eh, Thomas?'

'Neither of you gets much rest at weekends then?'

'Rest? You get a skinful of rest when you're dead, laddie. I'm out with the school football team on Saturday afternoons. Football team did I say? They lost again today. Raglan Street always loses. And it's only for want of football boots. If we had football boots we'd win. We had a centre forward last year – good kid he was – and he stole a pair of boots, and d'y'know we actually drew a couple of games. We could have won the last match but the police picked him up at half-time and dragged him away. And now he's in a reformatory school where they supply them with all the football gear they could wish for. He'll play for United in the years to come, mark my words. Ah, but man, you've got to keep turning out, haven't you?'

'Sunday?' asked Thomas.

'Ah, Sunday. Well, while Genghis here is getting 'em to sing "All Things Bright and Beautiful", I'm a sergeant-major at the Territorial Army barracks in Stretford Road, teaching 'em to march, salute, and stick bullets in their rifles. Saluting's the most important.'

'Are you expecting a war?' asked Thomas.

'Ach hell no, laddie; never in a million years. But for the out-of-works to get washed and shaved and dressed up in a uniform and marching away to a band makes a nice change for them after a week spent leaning on street corners, hands in their pockets, fags dangling from their mouths. I always tell the school-leavers to sign on for Sundays; if it does 'em no good, it'll do 'em no harm.'

Thomas shuffled his way along the wooden forms of the Boathouse Stadium. It was a barnlike building; the cold air was blue with tobacco smoke. There were more women in the audience than men, and young women at that; young women who wore belted raincoats and silk headscarves. They were not mill girls in shawls, nor miners' tarts; they were girls from the better districts of Withington and Didsbury who had gone to night school for

29

shorthand and typing and were now working as office girls in the city offices. Such a young woman took her place next to him.

In spite of his overcoat and her tight-belted raincoat, he could feel her body against his, or imagined he could. He glanced at her; she had a dainty face, a lovely face; she glanced at him, and he looked away quickly. She was the lass with the delicate air. She was the girl who could send him singing in the rain like in the song. She was Little Emily of *David Copperfield*, Estella of *Great Expectations*; she was Keats' lady in the meads who when she loved would make sweet moan; she was the bright innocent niece of a lord in a Wodehouse story. He glanced again; she almost smiled; he looked away.

He would have to think up a natural introduction. Perhaps a cigarette? He had five Woodbines in a paper packet, but they were being crushed between his hips and hers.

The wrestling began. Genghis Khan was booed, and Rob Roy cheered. They hoisted each other around the ring with the ease of sacks of feathers, but with the thuds of bags of coal. They fought like Titans fighting for command of the earth. Their bodies were wet and glistening with sweat. Thomas was amazed they could give and take such brutal treatment. Genghis kicked his knee in Rob Roy's back, and Rob Roy sank to his knees and howled as though his spine had been broken. But Rob Roy was up, and swung Genghis round and round, sending him flying with a smack into a corner post. Genghis held on to the ropes, and used both feet to send Rob Roy sprawling across the canvas. Genghis jumped on to Rob Roy's back, and Rob Roy's eyes looked up to heaven as though in death defeated. Somewhere from the back of the stadium a bagpipe began its discordant screeching. Genghis held his hands to his ears and appealed to the referee to stop the bagpipes. The referee refused. Rob Roy arched his back and held his hand to his ear to listen to the bagpipes. The people began stamping their feet.

The fair maid grabbed Thomas's shoulder and stood up. 'Put his bleeding head through the mangle! Rip his bloody balls off!' she shouted at the top of her voice. Thomas tried to sink his head down into his overcoat; he tried not to watch the violence in the ring; he tried not to hear the things she was shouting; more and more of her adjectives were effing and blinding. Most of the headscarved raincoated office girls were effing and blinding too.

It was not until he heard the crowd singing 'Will Ye No Come Back Again' that Thomas came out of his overcoat like a tortoise. Rob Roy, now wearing a bright kilt, was strutting around the ring. Genghis Khan the lay preacher was pretending to have had his arm broken; nevertheless, as he was being helped through the ropes, he swore that he would come back to fight Rob Roy another day and would gouge his eyes out. Rob Roy simply spat at him.

Thomas looked at the girl. Her eyes were wide and sparkling with the violence; her breasts were heaving. Thomas had an urge to kiss her.

'Can I walk you home?' he asked in a timid voice.

'No thank you,' she smiled sweetly. 'I'm not a twopenny-ha'penny tart you have up against a tree in the park.' And she was lost in the crowd.


The boil on the back of Liam's neck was nasty; it was large and red and sore; it was so painful he couldn't turn his head. His mother put a cushion on the table and gently lowered her son's head on it with a 'there there'. She beckoned for her husband to come and look at it.

'Aye?' she asked, raising her eyebrows in a question.

'Aye,' he said, nodding his head slowly in the affirmative.

'Now just sit ye comfortable in the chair and close your eyes, Liam me darlin',' she cooed to her son as she stroked his red curly hair.

The two parents busied themselves at the fire. She put handfuls of crumbled-up bread into a steaming cauldron and stirred it. The father wrapped the bottom half of a wide-brimmed bottle in a dirty towel and held the brim in the fire.

'And how's this new schoolmaster of yours?' asked the mother.

'He's sarky. It's not fair,' mumbled the boy. 'He doesn't give the strap. He gets them to laugh at you.'

'Sarky is he?' said his father, turning the bottle round in the fire. 'Now sure that's inhuman. Why can't he behave like a civilised gentleman and beat the bloody daylights out of yez like the last feller did? At least it'd give me the opportunity to go on up to the school and threaten to break his bloody jaw. Sure there's no answer to a man that's sarky, there is not.'

31

'But is he learning ye things?' asked the mother.

'Oh aye, he's interesting when he gets going, and you'd think he was Julius Caesar himself when he's telling you about the coming of the Romans. But he wants us to become clerks and wear white celluloid collars.'

'And don't ye know he may be right at that,' said the father, 'for there's more money to be earned sitting on your arse than ever there was spitting on your hands.'

'Will ye listen to your dad now, for 'tis the voice of wisdom speaking.'

'Would ye know, Liam me son, I could have become a rich and powerful doctor in the old country if only I'd been smitten with the reading and writing.'

'Did ye hear that now?' added the mother. 'And it's no semblance of a lie your dad's telling ye at all. Sure there wasn't a man in the length and breadth of Ireland as could wring the neck of a hen or slaughter a fattened pig as deftly as could yer dad. Ach, he was renowned.'

'Aye, that I was. But 'twas the booklearning as let me down. D'y'know, I'd never heard of Julius Caesar, not a word.' The man nodded towards his son's neck.

'Aye?' he asked his wife, raising his eyebrows, in question.

'Aye,' she replied, nodding her head slowing in the affirmative.

He took the hot bottle from the fire and put the rim down on the lad's boil, giving the bottom of the bottle a slap with his hand. There was an explosive squelch and the bottle filled with yellow pus and red blood. The boy screamed and passed out.

His mother scooped the boiling bread from the cauldron and wrapped it in an old shirt on the table.

'I'll be after putting the bread poultice on his neck before he comes out of his faint,' she said. 'D'y'think he'll be fit for school in the morning?'

'If he isn't, I'll be wanting to know why.'

32

Thomas's mother was upset and trembling. She wandered around the rooms like a demented soul, flicking through book after book; she had romance novels everywhere, they lay at random wherever she left them, on things, under things, behind things.

'Oh dear, Thomas, I can't find the gas bill, and they'll send me to prison.'

'Of course they won't, mom.'

'I've got the money for it; you know I have. I put it by every week, and I keep it in the cup without the handle under my bed. But it's the bill; I can't find the bill. They'll lock me up.'

'All you've got to do is go down to the town hall with the money.'

'It's either with Ruby Ayres or Ethel M. Dell. Ah!' She pulled an envelope from one of the books. 'Here it is, and in Ethel M. Dell. She's a sneaky one is Ethel M. Dell; she had it all the time. If she does it again I won't read any more of her books.'

'Mom, you should stop using letters as bookmarks. I wouldn't mind, but you forget which book you're reading and just pick up another and carry on reading.' Thomas laughed. 'Anyway, you can thank Ethel M. Dell for giving you a happy ending. You won't have to go to prison. I'm off. I'll be late.'

But Thomas was in time to see the worst playground fight since he'd started at Raglan Street. There was shouting, swearing, kicking, thumping and the throwing of half bricks; there was scratching, tearing, twisting and head butting; blood everywhere.

Dick Wilson and Charlie Macgregor watched from the window.

'What's going on?' asked Thomas.

'Now's the day, and now's the hour; see the front o' battle lour!' said Charlie.

''Tis the game of Prohibition they're playing – '

'Playing?'

'The one lot is the Chicago Irish, and the other is the Chicago Italians.'

'Shouldn't we try to stop it?'

'Ach no, me fine feller, this is a game; it's contained; it's a safety valve; stops 'em getting too serious. Keep it in the play-ground, don't let it get on the streets, for in the streets there can be a killing, and that's a fact so it is.'

Dick Wilson poured himself out a drink; the other two refused when he waved the bottle towards them. He looked at his waist-coat watch: 'Just a few minutes more!'

Miss Cowgill skipped in, oblivious to the noise of battle.

'And away to the maypole high,' she sang. Then she skipped out again tra-la-la-ing Mozart's *Eine Kleine Nachtmusik*.

Dick blew the whistle immediately the minute hand jerked to nine o'clock, and the inevitable clog-clattering boot-banging stampede burst into the corridor. Ten boys had to limp off to the clinic with bleeding gashes on their heads and faces.

Thomas went to his first classroom as soon as the thumping of boots turned into a clattering of desk lids. He had barely turned into the room when he heard:

Golden slumbers kiss your eyes,
   Smiles await you when you rise;
Sleep, pretty wantons, do not cry,
   And I will sing a lullaby.

This was too much for him to believe. He had to see for him-self. He peeped into the hall, and the sight was beyond belief. Miss Cowgill was a little fat queen in command. Fifty injured scholars stood in straight rows before her, and she waved her knitting needle like a fairy wand. She could get Satan to sing psalms. It was magic.

There was more magic over the tea and arrowroot biscuit at playtime; but it was a magic he had half expected, like Ebeneezer Scrooge knew he would be visited by the final spirit.

'Would you care to accompany me to a cinema on Saturday evening?' she asked him. Half expected, but not fully expected; he had expected to be introduced to her sideline for he'd realised now that all schoolteachers had sidelines; he'd not expected to be invited out on a date, if it was a date. He said yes without embarrassment or shyness; it was, he guessed, a ritual invitation like the ones from Dick and Charlie had been.

He was to meet her outside the Coronation Picture Palace, known she told him as the Cosy Corry, in Northenden. Northenden again! Perhaps all schoolteachers were supposed to live in Northenden, only nobody had told him at the interview.

'The only way I'll leave this house will be feet first,' said his mother when he put the suggestion of moving to her. 'Your father bought this house for us to live in when Moss Side was the district of the gentry. There were doctors and architects – '

'And an aviator who waved to a German baron from his aeroplane,' snarled Thomas.

'There's no need to be sarcastic with your mother. Is that what they taught you at university?' She started to polish the sideboard vigorously. 'Honour thy father and mother that thy days may be long in the land.'

'But suppose I'd taken a job at one of those posh public schools like in *The Magnet* and *The Gem* as you'd hoped. Would you have stayed here on your own?'

She sniffed her tin of polish. 'That would have been different. I could have lived near the school in a country cottage with a tiled floor and a log fire and oil lamps and an owl in the tree and all smelling of real lavender from the garden, not this waxed stuff out of a tin.' She slammed the tin down. 'And the woman in the shop charged me a penny more than she should have done for it. "But it's the best wax polish," she said. "I don't care if it was made by queen bees," I said.'

Thomas went into the scullery to put fresh carbide in his bicycle lamp ready for the ride to Northenden. He was excited yet afraid of meeting Miss Cowgill. She was small and round, a roly-poly pudding and pie woman. She was about the same age as his mother, but she had a feminine smell; not a lavender wax polish smell, a clean apron smell, a bacon and egg smell or a disinfectant smell like his mother, but a woman smell. But would Miss Cowgill expect him to do it to her; to make love to her and that? He couldn't; he wouldn't be able to; she was too fat, too old. He felt nothing physical happen to him when he thought about her, and yet he'd gone physical at just the fantasy of meeting a non-existent girl. He had never been out with any girl before, although he was always thinking about it and hoping for it, especially when he lay in bed at night. But the naked girl who came to his imagination was pale, slim yet shapely, and enchanting; full beautiful, a fairy's child with long hair and dainty feet and wild wild eyes. No, he wouldn't be able to do it with Miss Cowgill, but he was convinced she would expect it of him. What would her reaction be when he couldn't do it? Would she sing a mocking song? He could not back down from the invitation. He would have to meet her come what may!

He chained his bicycle to some iron railings and waited outside the Cosy Corry. It was the smallest picturedrome he'd ever seen. It had never grown up into a cinema, and never would; it was stunted. It was still showing silent films even though other cinemas had gone over to talkies a few years ago. Miss Cowgill waddled towards him, took him by the arm and led him inside. They didn't have to pay even though he had the money in his hand. He'd been a shilling short, but he'd borrowed it from his mother's gas cup without the handle, without his mother knowing; he couldn't have told her he was a shilling short of his picture money to take a girl.

'Evening, Bessie!' the ticket girl nodded.

'Evening, Bessie!' smiled the usherette, giving Miss Cowgill a nudge with her elbow. 'Got a feller, eh?'

'They call me Bessie after Bessie Bunter,' she told him. 'But I don't mind. It's their little joke. And it's better than being called baby hippo.'

She led him to the very front, the screen was way up above them, and they sat down on the end of a wooden form near the piano. He could hear the shuffling of feet as the picturedrome began to fill up, and the smell of orange peel mixed with the smell of freshly lighted cigarettes. He was too embarrassed to look around; people would think he was with her, and they were seated on the twopenny form. People would laugh.

'I suppose you've been to a club with Mr Wilson?' she whispered.

'Yes.'

'He's very funny. And you'll have been to the wrestling with Mr Macgregor?'

'Yes.'

'He's very strong and very brave. Well now you'll see my little out-of-hours activity. It keeps the big bad wolf from the door.

Enjoy yourself, Mr Davies.'

She slid off the end of the form and took her place at the piano. The first film was Tom Mix with Cowboys and Indians. Miss Cowgill alternated between Rossini's William Tell Overture and Chopin's Turkish March, changing tempo from trot to gallop as the action demanded.

Then came the interval, and she continued playing, but now her songs were the popular ones of the day, and the audience sang to them. The lights were on, and Thomas wished he could disappear; even more so did he want to vanish into thin air when she brought him into the songs. When 'Carolina Moon' reached 'shining, shining on the one that I adore', she looked straight at him and blew him a kiss. The audience whistled and shouted 'yoo-hoo!'

The worst was to come for Thomas in the feature film. It was Garbo and Gilbert, and was full of horrible kissing; horrible because Garbo didn't know when to stop kissing, and Thomas wondered if he might be expected to do the same, especially after the blown kiss in 'Carolina Moon' and her pretending to look for bubbles above his head in 'I'm Forever Blowing Bubbles'. A sneaky glance behind him showed that most of the audience seemed to be kissing when Garbo kissed. To these scenes Miss Cowgill played Chopin's Fantasie Impromptu.

The ticket girl gave her half a crown on their way out; it was her fee for the night. She guided him through the narrow streets of Northenden, turn left, turn right, down the passageway, cross the road, now left, now right. They came to her cottage.

It was a tiny cottage pressed between newly built houses. Ivy held to the wall around the doorway; the two small windows were latticed; the fence was wooden; it was right for Miss Cowgill. It had been left by mother to mother to mother to her, she told him.

Inside, she closed the red velvet curtains and lit two rose-designed oil lamps. She put him to sit on an upright wooden chair near the piano, near the piano again; and within a few minutes she was playing and singing to him, with little actions to the songs, like pretending to scan the horizon during 'One Friday Morn' or wiping tears from her eyes in 'Early One Morning' or wagging her finger in rebuke for 'No, John, No'. His lungs ached for a cigarette, but he dared not interrupt to ask for permission to smoke. His back was aching; he'd been sitting upright without a

37

back rest in the Cosy Corry. There was a crick in his neck through holding his head back to look at the screen. He slowly realised he wanted to urinate, and tried desperately to put the idea out of his mind. It was boring. It was endless.

And then Miss Cowgill began playing the Fantasie Impromptu and he became afraid. He was convinced this was his cue, an undeniable invitation to kiss her. But he couldn't kiss her. But he'd have to kiss her. He braced himself to put his hands on her shoulders and kiss the back of her neck. She would turn to him with puckered lips; he would close his eyes and kiss her lips with his lips. Before he could bat an eyelid, she slammed the piano lid down and wagged her finger at him. 'Now, now, Mr Davies! Naughty-naughty! I think it's time I sent you on your merry way.'

What had he done? He hadn't moved! And she had her back to him! She couldn't have read his mind; people couldn't do things like that. Had he said something rude without knowing it?

'You're an awfully nice young man,' she said. 'And I invited you home to sing and play for you; well, not exactly for you, but you'll not understand. It was very courteous of you to be my companion at the Coronation Picture Palace, Mr Davies, and I was grateful for your support. I am indebted to you for sitting through my little home-made concert, and I hope I may have entertained you. Now, please leave, Mr Davies, before your primitive passions get the better of you.' She pushed him out into the black night. He had to run down a passageway and urinate; the noise seemed very loud, and he thought he would never stop. He was sure people would come out of their houses.

It took him a long time to find which railings in which street he'd chained his bicycle to. He wandered lost through a maze of strange lanes before he found his bike. The wind blew out many matches before he was able to get the carbide to flare.

He was hungry. He'd only had melody and song all evening, and his stomach rumbled. He bought some fish and chips in a newspaper and leaned over the Mersey bridge to eat them. The river was black below him. There was no moon, but a few gas lamps made yellow shimmers. On his left was a glow of the city lamps on the clouds; on his right the blackness of a Cheshire night. He wiped his greasy fingers on his handkerchief, crumpled up the newspaper, and dropped it over the bridge to float away to Liverpool. The Fantasie Impromptu ran through his brain. He was in love, but not with Miss Cowgill, for who could ever be in love with Miss Cowgill? Yet an evening in the company of a woman, any woman, had sparked off this love he now felt for nobody, for a dream woman. Something in the music and the nearness to a female had triggered off instincts he'd only ever read about; he'd read about romance, not in his own books, but in snatched glances he'd stolen from his mother's romances while she was cooking in the scullery. He was in love with romance. Perhaps some wisp of a ghost maiden, wearing only a gown of gossamer and surrounded by an irresistible perfume beyond myrrh, might rise up from the river and pull him down into the black water. He frightened himself that it might really happen, and rode his bicycle off the bridge as fast as he could, not feeling safe and real until he came to a lamppost.

'I bought you the latest Sexton Blake,' said his mother when she brought his malted milk to his bedroom. 'I've been very lonely, but I don't mind as long as you're out enjoying yourself.'

'Thank you, mom.'

She bent down and gave him a quick goodnight kiss on his forehead. Then she stepped back suddenly.

'Thomas, have you been out with a woman? Don't lie to me, Thomas.'

'No, mom!' He felt his denial was possibly true. 'Why?'

'Because you have the look of a man who has been in the company of a woman, that's all.'

'Smell me. You can't smell perfume.'

'I'm so glad,' she smiled. 'Women only want what money they can get out of a man. And it would be a shame after the way I've scrimped and saved to put you through university for a woman to come along and take your hard-earned money off you. Though, heaven forbid, you don't bring home much. It's a good job I don't charge you rent and keep like some mothers do. Just a few shillings, that's all I ever ask from you. There are some Jezebels who lead a man to borrow money or even steal money.'

'Don't worry, mom,' said Thomas, and he scratched through the Sexton Blake as though desperately anxious to start reading it.

'Funny thing,' said his mother as she went out through the door. 'I keep all my money in little pots throughout the house. I check them every evening. And there's a shilling missing from the cup without the handle.'

As soon as she'd left the room, he put his head under the blankets and made a tent with his knees. It was safe and secure in that black tent, especially knowing the light was burning outside. Thomas felt inadequate; inadequate as a schoolmaster; inadequate as a man.


There was the usual violence in the early morning playground; mob against mob; fists, boots, bricks and the occasional flash of a knife. There was blood. But there had been worse battles in the past.

'Would ye know, and I'm thinking the standard of culture among the scholars is improving,' said Dick Wilson, indicating the carnage through the window with his cup of whiskey. 'For 'tis Romans and Britons they're fighting at now. When ye first came, Thomas, 'twas Al Capone every morning. Ah, sure there'll be the same number of little sods heading for the clinic with their wounds, but, no, I detect a distinct uplift in culture.'

'Next week it'll be Normans and Saxons,' laughed Thomas.

'Aye, well as long as ye steer well clear of the Battle of the Boyne.'

'Or Culloden,' added Charlie Macgregor.

Whether due to Thomas's influence or not, the school had shown a slight cultural lift within a few months. Charlie Macgregor took the whistle out into the playground. The first whistle was for scholars to stand to attention; the second for them to run into class lines; the third for them to march into the school. Dick Wilson had obtained a gramophone with an extra large horn. On the first whistle he wound the gramophone up; on the second he put a military march record on; with the third blast he put the needle head down to play. And only then did he pour himself out a whiskey, not counting a first introductory whiskey.

'Aye, there's a touch o' cultural uplift come sneaking in,' he went on. 'For instance, Thomas, I've noticed a more legible hand in their sick notes. Sure they still write the things themselves for none of their parents can read or write, but the writing is becoming copperplate, and would ye know I'm beginning to enjoy reading their imaginative excuses. Wasn't there a note only yesterday signed "Doctor Virgil"?'

40

The reason was simple enough. In order that they could not cheat by guessing what letters and words were coming next, Thomas filled the blackboard with copperplate Latin from Virgil. Each thin upstroke and thick downstroke had therefore to be copied with absolute accuracy. As a reward he translated Virgil for them afterwards, although it wasn't strictly Virgil; he read them the funnier passages from P. G. Wodehouse and W. W. Jacobs.

'But there's just one wee complaint I have with ye, me fine broth of a boy,' said Dick Wilson. He pointed to Friday on the pinned up timetable. 'As ye've noticed, there's just one word written across all Friday and that's "Scripture". Well now, I know Fridays are free to do what the hell ye like with. In the junior schools they bring their books and toys; ah but can't ye imagine what toys this lot would bring with 'em, eh? Knuckledusters and catapults, eh? Sure lessons are finished for the week, and we chalk it up to Scripture for the simple reason we're supposed to ram a bit of scripture down their throats from time to time; the Education Committee down at the town hall likes the idea. Mind you, I'm not qualified to teach scriptures.'

'Do you want me to teach scripture?'

'Ach, I'm not saying ye should and I'm not saying ye shouldn't. Me wee complaint with ye is not what ye teach but how ye teach it. I'm surprised ye've not noticed before the subtle difference of Fridays. I'll be having a wee word with ye on the subject after today's performance.'

Charlie Macgregor went out to blow the whistles, and Dick began to wind the gramophone up. Since the military marches had started, Miss Cowgill no longer popped her head in the office with a sunny quotation; she no longer tra-la-la-ed the light fantastic up the corridor to a lively little classic; she sat alone at the piano in the hall and waited for lessons to begin. It was guessed she didn't like military music as not being her kind of music.

'Now if only Sousa would write something like the march of the cuckoos or buttercups on parade we might still be getting the merry morning madrigals,' said Dick.

Thomas went to his classroom feeling almost as lonely as Miss Cowgill seemed to be. He was perplexed over his headmaster's mild rebuke. He wrote GOD in large letters across the black-

41

board.

'Please, sir,' said Hetherard Saar, one of the German boys, 'is God like me?'

'I think it's supposed to be the other way round, Saar. It is believed we are made in his image, although whether you are included in the "we" I wouldn't know.'

'Then does he have a bum, sir?'

'Alker is the expert on that subject. Ask him.'

'I think he must have a bum, sir. Though he usually has it covered in a long nightdress for photographs,' said Alker.

'Then he must go out to the lavatory in the back yard like us, sir,' went on Saar. 'Remember, sir? You showed us one of his turds last week when you took us out in the playground. Only you said it was the airship R101 flying over Manchester. It was shaped like a turd, wasn't it, sir. And Ancoats is God's shithouse. And when it rains, it's God pulling the chain.'

There was a burst of laughter, and Saar looked around, proud of himself. Thomas retreated from the room.

Where e'er you walk, cool gales shall fan the glade;
Trees where you sit shall crowd into a shade.

His boys were ready to riot; Miss Cowgill's, the same kind of boys, were blissfully singing another cissie song. Saar had challenged him with his crude wit. If he used the strap on Saar, which he felt like doing for the first time since he'd started school, the action of violence would turn him into an ordinary schoolmaster like they'd been used to. Victory would be theirs; defeat would be his; his days at the school could be numbered.

There was silence when he returned to the classroom. They were watching and waiting.

'You seem to be an expert in religious matters, Saar.'

'Yes, sir.'

'Good. That's more than I am. So come out to the front, will you?' Saar strode out, gripping his hands above his head like a winning prizefighter, smiling at the class.

'Indeed, you have such a talent in that direction that I'm going to make you Archbishop of Canterbury.'

'Thank you, sir.' The boy gave another victory grip.

'Fine. Then you can be Thomas à Becket. And I shall be King

42

Henry the Second, how's that?'

'I don't mind, sir.'

Thomas chalked up names and dates as he spoke.

'I'm a good king. I came to the throne in 1154, and I died in 1189.' There were cheers from the class on the word 'died'.

'I ruled over England and parts of France. I subdued the Irish and brought them under English rule.' This time there were boos from the class.

'I was very concerned with legal reform and I worked hard for good government. Unfortunately I had a lot of trouble from my Archbishop of Canterbury, Thomas à Becket here. Give them a big smile and a victory clench, Your Grace!' Saar did so, but he looked less confident. 'I wore the crown, but he wanted to be boss, he thought he could pit his wits against mine, which was rather stupid of him. However, I was surrounded by strong and loyal knights.' He waved his arms to the class. 'I appoint you my reliable knights.' The lads stuck their thumbs in the lapels of their jackets and did boastful Irish sways. 'Well, I tell you, I'd just about had it up to my neck with this smart alec Archbishop, and in a fit of annoyance I said to my sturdy knights – "Who will rid me of this turbulent priest?" And do you know what they did? They rode all the way to Canterbury and killed him, killed him stone dead; which wasn't very nice of them. However, he was turned into a saint, and people made pilgrimages to the cathedral in which he was murdered. In a way, it was the beginning of English literature because Geoffrey Chaucer was inspired to write *The Canterbury Tales* in 1386. Thomas à Becket was murdered on December 29th in the year 1170. I shall expect you to remember all these names and dates. It's nearly playtime, so you can go early.' He put his arm around Saar's shoulder. 'This blessed boy, who is more holy than any of you, can go first. Nip along, Your Grace, and try to find a hiding place if you can.'

'What in the name of all that's holy and wonderful is going on out there now?' asked Dick Wilson, handing a cup of whiskey to Thomas, who took it without realising he was taking it.

There was a rough-house in the playground. Fists were flying like windmills.

'It's their enthusiasm for ecclesiastical history,' said Thomas. 'They're canonising Saar.'

'Canonising is it? And them pulling his trousers off.'

43

'They have their own way of doing things in Ancoats.'

'Ah, me bright spalpeen, ye're learning fast. But, tell me, did ye learn what ye were doing wrong on Fridays?'

'Yes. Teaching scripture.'

'Ah, sure that's not it, not at all. Nobody teaches scripture. Thomas, me boy, it's surprised I am that a young man with your obvious keen powers of perception has not observed what's before your very eyes. Will ye look at me now? And will ye cast your eyes on Charlie Macgregor? Ye'll see we're both wearing the tweed sports jacket. Every schoolmaster in the civilised world and beyond wears a tweed sports jacket on Friday. And there's you in your black suit as if you were going to a funeral. Tweeds, Thomas – tweeds. The scholars expect it of us. Even Miss Cowgill wears a tweed skirt.'

'This is the only suit I've got. I can't afford a tweed jacket.'

'Sure that's no excuse. Where there's a will, eh, Thomas? The people round here can't afford to live, but somehow they manage it. Just ye get a tweed jacket for Fridays and I won't care if ye teach devil worship to the little sods.'

# The busy whisper

It was getting dark. The glass side of the street gas lamp had been smashed; the gas mantle had also been smashed, and there was merely a tiny blue flame which popped and spluttered, throwing no light at all. A little brown Italian girl dawdled up the street. She sucked a thin stick of black liquorice, looking at it between sucks to see how shiny it was. The two lads darted out of the entry, grabbed her and pulled her into the drain-stinking blackness.

'Hey, hey, hey! What you do? Let me go! Where me dad? Dad! Wanna go home! Let-a me go home! Go way, go way!'

'We're going to feel up your clothes,' said Keenan. 'It won't hurt. You'll like it. They all do.'

'Me daddy! Me daddy!' Her cries stopped suddenly when Kelly smashed his fist into her face and held his hand over her mouth. She made stifled bubbling noises.

Keenan knelt down and tried to force her legs apart. She struggled to keep her legs tightly together.

'I'll break your bloody legs if you don't open them,' snarled Keenan.

Eventually he was able to part her feet, and he kept them apart with his knees. She still struggled, but he pulled her knickers down her legs and over her shoes. He played with her with his finger.

The whistle of a train on the main line frightened them. They left the little girl and ran into the street and down the street.

'Hey, me knickers! You gotta me knickers! Give me my knickers! Me mamma she ask!'

'Tell her you gave 'em to a boy for a stick of liquorice,' shouted Keenan. 'We're going to put them through the priest's letterbox so he can bless them.'

'Yeh!' said Kelly, excited at the thought.

'I know the school you go! I tell the new teacher! You all afraid of him! I tell him!'

45

'Then bloody tell him!' Keenan shouted back. The lads ran down the street until they felt safe.

'She might, y'know,' said Kelly. 'She might tell Davies.'

'He won't bother,' said Keenan. 'He's a nancy-boy. Nancy-boys don't care what happens to girls.'

'A what?'

'A nancy-boy, a bum-boy, a meg-harry; he'd rather kiss a feller than kiss a tart. Have ye not heard about them?'

'How d'y'know he's a meg-harry?'

'Cos he smells of perfume.'

'Does he buggery!'

'Well, he smells clean then, and it's the same thing. Wilson smells of booze; Scotts Porridge smells of sweat; Miss Cowshit smells of tit; but Mavis smells clean. That's how I know. Sides, suppose he was to find out. Sure what'd he do? He'd be dead sarky, and then he'd tell us about Joan of Arc getting burned at the stake or summat.'


By arrangement, Thomas joined Dick and his wife Kitty outside a church hall in Fallowfield. They waited in a queue for fifteen minutes until the doors were unbolted for a jumble sale.

''Tis the age-old system of barter,' Dick explained. 'People chuck in their old and unwanted clothes, and other people fight over 'em for a few coppers. Course this is a middle-class district, and ye have to pretend the clothes ye snatch are for your gardener or odd-job man, ye say it in a loud voice while ye're tussling with somebody else like two birds over a worm. Now me darling Kitty here is a fully qualified jumbler, and ye'd go a long way to find three kids as well dressed as ours. And have ye ever seen me looking shabby? Sure that's thanks to Kitty's sharp eyes, me own darling Kitty.' He gave her a hug even though they were in a queue of strangers.

Kitty indeed had the appearance of a first class rummager. She had a long sharp nose which gave her the look of a bird; her eyes switched hither and thither like birds' eyes. As they stood waiting, she glanced sharply at a passing tram car; stared at it as though taking in every detail of the driver, guard and passengers. Then, with a swift jerk of her head, she concentrated on a cat. A second later, with a sudden movement of her eyes, she was

46

staring into the face of a sailor on a cigarette packet which had been thrown on to the pavement. She carried three neatly folded canvas bags, giving one to Thomas and one to her husband.

The doors opened wide and people fought and pushed to get inside the hall. Thomas was carried in the stream like a crumpled newspaper in the flow of the Mersey. He managed to get out of the current and into a quiet corner which was dominated by a large framed picture of a white missionary in the jungle handing a bible to a very happy and delighted little black child. From here he was able to observe Kitty in action. She grabbed clothing without appearing to look at what she'd got. She handed over pennies, and she pushed her purchases deep into her bag. She elbowed from table to table. Dick was doing the same at the book table, although with not quite the same alacrity.

Thomas was bewildered by the noise of shuffling feet and the waving of many arms; most of the people seemed to have four or five arms. He stared up at the stern face of the missionary until Kitty grabbed his arm and steered him through a tidal wave of women to a table heaped high with men's clothes. She pulled and tugged at a tweed sleeve which was hanging out from near the bottom of the pile.

'There y'are now, 'tis just the thing for that gardener of yours. 'Twill last him a lifetime,' she shouted in a loud voice. 'And will ye look at the label; 'tis the orb and cross; 'tis genuine Harris tweed made by islanders of the wind-swept Hebrides.'

Seconds later, when she had paid threepence for it, she whispered: ''Tis just your very size; you'll find 'tis a perfect fit.' Dick put his arm lovingly around Kitty's shoulders; his eyes were full of admiration for her. 'Now isn't she the one, eh, Thomas? Sure that jacket will last ye a thousand Fridays. It'll make a big difference to your scriptures, see if it doesn't.'

Thomas had been invited back to tea with them, and it was therefore taken for granted he would be Mick going round with the hat for Paddy at some club later that night.

It was a comfortable home overlooking Birchfields Park; trees could be seen through the window. There was a warm, red and flame-dancing fire which made the brassware, and there were lots of brasses, sparkle; each piece of brass ornament was polished almost white, like a tram car handle, which was polished by a turning glove for twenty hours a day. There was a painting, which Thomas guessed was Ireland, of a whitewashed rock cottage and a man leading a donkey towards it; there was a green sea and blue mountains.

Their three children were well behaved and spoke only when spoken to. They squatted on the carpet before the fire sorting out the items which their parents had brought back for them; a doll with an arm missing and a doll's house without a roof for the little girl; a wooden fort without a tower and an assortment of lead soldiers and farmyard animals, all with things like legs, tails and rifles missing, for the youngest boy; and a chess set for the oldest boy, although he had to do a deal with his brother in order to borrow a cow without a leg for the white king and a soldier without a head for the black bishop. There were also jigsaw puzzles and lots of books. After tea the children took their treasures up to their rooms.

'Would ye have a cup of tea before ye set off on your travels,' said Kitty. 'I'd offer ye something stronger but neither Dick nor I touch alcohol in any shape or form.'

'Yes, please,' said Thomas. He was surprised, and Dick jumped up to say he'd put some more coal on the fire; the fire didn't need any more coal, it was blazing away.

'Do ye like teaching at Raglan Street?' asked Kitty.

'Yes. Very much.'

'Are ye a Catholic?'

'No.'

'Dick's a Catholic. I'm a Protestant.'

'Good. I'm glad to hear that.'

'Why?'

'Because I like people to differ.'

'We had to come to England to get married. They don't like people to differ in Ireland; only in the price of pigs in the market. We were married in a registry office, and Holy Mother Church has officially excommunicated me for living in sin. Aye, excommunicated! Course I can get off the blooming hook if I confess to living in sin, and the two of us, like a couple of penitents, get married again in a Catholic church, but sure 'tis not worth the blather. I loved this good woman here, and I married her legally, and I still love her and always will.'

'Ach, ye daft galoot!' said Kitty, and she got up to put coal on the fire.

'And ye might as well hear the rest. Me grandfather – me father's father – was hanged by the British for being Irish. And Kitty's father was shot by the Irish for being a Loyalist. And here's me the headmaster of a Saxon school with hardly a single Saxon among the scholars. So would ye not say, Thomas, that we're typically Irish, the pair of us?'

'Are you Welsh, Thomas?' asked Kitty.

'I don't honestly know.'

'Only Thomas Davies is a Welsh name, so it is.'

'I suppose so. I don't feel English.'

'If you're wishful to know whether you're a Celt or not,' said Dick, filling his pipe, 'consult an oak tree, talk to a wren, ask a salmon; they'll tell ye. And right now I'm telling ye that if we don't want to be roasted like oxen on a spit we'd be advised to pull our chairs back from the fire.'

The cat didn't mind the heat of the fire; it stretched full length on the rug. The clock chimed a comfortable Westminster chime. Dick lit his pipe.

'And that's something else,' he said. 'We'll have to get you started on a pipe instead o' them daft little rolled up bits of paper. Ye've got the Scottish tweed to go with an Irish briar.'

There was a brief moment, a warm timeless moment, when Dick went out of the room to get the hats and coats. Kitty held Thomas by the hand.

'Find yourself a woman to love, Thomas,' she said, 'and settle down to a married life, for it doesn't do for a man to live his life out on his own in a world of children. Things can go wrong.' And then she straightaway reached for the poker to poke the fire as though she had said nothing at all. Dick was back in a jiffy.

The jacket needed a bit of sponging, a bit of darning, a bit of airing, all of which Kitty promised to have done for Thomas by the time they got back from the ramblings of Paddy Reilly.

It was a good night at the Flying Angel, a seaman's club by the Ship Canal. Paddy Reilly was in good form, and Mick's hat was filled with coins, although most of them were foreign.

Thomas cycled home late with his cleaned and repaired tweed jacket all neatly tied in a bundle behind the saddle. It was draped over a chair in the bedroom when his mother came in with his goodnight sleep-tight steaming drink. She stood in the room like a stately ghost of a lady long ago.

49

'What on earth is that?' she asked.

'Got it at a jumble sale for threepence,' said Thomas.

'Then it can go right in the dustbin where it belongs. It'll be crawling with lice, as if you don't bring enough home as it is. Whatever will they think round here?'

'They won't know it's from a jumble sale. How could they?' Thomas was beginning to tense up. She was saying exactly what he'd known she'd say.

'You never know what they can find out. Moss Side used to be such a nice district, but there's some strange people moving in these days. They find out things. And somebody wearing somebody else's cast-offs is just the very thing they're waiting to talk about.'

'I'm sorry, mother; I'm keeping it, and I'm wearing it for scriptures.' He felt himself tightening up like elastic.

She stood back shocked. 'I see. It's mother now, is it? What's happened to mom? Is that what university taught you? To hurt your mother's feelings? To ride roughshod? It's as well your father never came back to witness this.'

'Oh, shit-a-brick!!' shouted Thomas. And then he wanted to jump through the window. His mother said nothing for a long time; she just stood there.

'I have never heard such filthy language in all my born days. And coming from the mouth of my own son. I thought it was your job to teach the gutter rats, but it seems they're teaching you. And I vowed and declared I'd never mention the matter, but even though the shilling mysteriously reappeared in the cup without the handle I know it was missing for an entire evening. It was stolen by a thief, and that thief is in this very room at this very moment.'

She disappeared from the room.

Thomas made a black tent with his knees and slid down under the blankets.

In the morning, Thomas fully expected to be greeted with a stern silence, broken occasionally by sniffs, sobs and the banging of cupboard doors. That's how it usually was when his mother was in a temper. Instead, she was gentle:

'There you are, Thomas, I managed to get some brown sugar for your porridge because I know you like brown sugar.' She pushed the sugar bowl across the table to him. 'But I had to trudge from shop to shop to get it. Believe me, my feet were aching. I shall have to get my feet seen to; they get very sore. Not all shops sell brown sugar; it's dearer than white. And while you're at school I'll sponge that tweed jacket with disinfectant.'

'Thank you, mom!'

'Oh, and do you know what, Thomas? That naughty Ethel M. Dell has done it again; she's a sly little puss is that one. I found this letter in one of her books. I don't suppose it's important.'

It was a letter from the grammar school offering him a position. But it was six months old. The grammar school would think he hadn't had the courtesy to reply. Perhaps he would have taken the job; perhaps he wouldn't. It was too late anyway.

The university was on his way to school; from there he turned up Brunswick Street through Ardwick and into Ancoats. He always stopped for a few seconds to say 'good morning' to Owens College. Across Oxford Road and facing the quadrangle gate was the College Inn; next to that up Brunswick Street was a dowdy little shop with 'Prof. Eldo Rhado, Phrenologist' painted on its dirty window. Inside the window was a large wax model of a head, twice as big as an ordinary head, marked out in many sections like fields as seen from a mountain; each section was marked with an attribute like 'mathematics', 'science', 'painting', 'Plato', and even 'Love of Jesus'. The professor's wife was Princess Eldo Rhado, and she read palms. An additional service the little shop offered was its display of postcard advertisements, usually from graduates or failures selling their books: 'Gray's

Anatomy. Cheap. Apply Within' or 'Complete Works of William Shakespeare. Hardly Used. Apply Within'. These were usually interspersed with 'Good Home Sought for Kitten' or 'Comfortable Lodgings for Students. Irish navvies need Not Apply'. Most students had visited this shop to have their bumps felt or their palms read; none of them ever believed the nonsense, and it was usually the result of a dare. Next door, conveniently, was the beerhouse where they could obtain courage to step inside the shop, and also visit it afterwards in order to celebrate the news that they were going to graduate and then become rich and famous and live a long life. Thomas looked at the giant head in the window. He didn't believe, but how he wished somebody would dare him to go in and have his fortune told; he needed to know something about himself even if it was only a pack of lies.

The letter from the grammar school had made him feel he was wasting his time at Raglan Street. All he had done was instil a form of discipline by using a form of sarcasm; he had taught them nothing. Like Dick had said, his main purpose was to distribute free milk until the boys were old enough to hold their caps out for national assistance money. All that rubbish about archbishops and kings was merely teaching born losers about born winners; the propaganda of the conquerors. He tore the letter up and dropped the pieces down a grid, and cycled on.

As he turned from Pin Mill Brow into Every Street, it struck him like a sledgehammer. It was there in front of him; he couldn't miss it; and yet he'd been passing it for months without even thinking. There was the Horsfall Museum, a soot-caked Elizabethan manor house, a building of excellent shape standing among the huge mills, shadowed by a forest of high mill chimneys. It was something he was sure he could use, and it was less than a minute from his blackboard.

He propped his bike on the steps and walked in. A woman stepped out of the shadows and frightened him for a second.

'I thought you were a burglar,' she said; 'they're the only kind of people likely to come in here on a nice day.'

She was Miss Hindshaw, the curator, a middle-aged lady with kind eyes in a face as brown and wrinkled as a papyrus scroll, yet there was the beauty of quality in her face.

'When it's bitter cold, people come in for the warmth. Hot air comes up through the grids in the floor from the coke furnace.

They sometimes fight each other to stand on the grids.'

'I'd like to bring classes of boys, not necessarily for the warmth,' said Thomas, explaining who he was and what he did.

'Please do. That's what it's here for. Do you know anything about the museum?'

'I'm sorry. I er...'

'Don't worry; nobody ever does. Well, it was, as you can see, an Elizabethan Hall, occupied for centuries by the Mosley family. No doubt it once stood with grace and beauty among the green meadows leading down to the River Medlock, which would have had its share of trout. Today I believe the river is well stocked with dead cats and dogs, the meadows have been covered in verminous hovels, and the trees have been replaced by factory chimneys. Bonnie Prince Charlie stayed here when he took Manchester, so you might say it was once fit for a king. John Byrom spent weekends here; quite possibly he saluted a few happy morns from these windows. Then in 1886, Thomas Horsfall bought it to turn into a people's palace. He was backed by Ruskin and Lord Leighton, and they picked what they considered the worst slum area in Britain to fill with copies of art treasures. They hoped to make people dissatisfied with their conditions by showing them a better way of life, a life enjoyed by the rich. They bought copies of Turner's paintings to show the people that there were other landscapes than mills and factories; they added pictures of birds, butterflies, trees, lakes, mountains and the sea to show the children of the slums things they had never seen in real life, and perhaps never would. There was a room for classical music to be played if musicians could be tempted to make their sounds for nothing. There was a room done up like a working class home to show that there could be artistic taste even in ordinary cups and saucers, furniture and wallpaper. And there's this room...'

She unlocked a door and led him into what had been the banqueting hall. 'You'll understand why I keep it under lock and key,' she smiled. The room was filled with larger than life-sized copies of the Greek sculptures; of the ancient gods and goddesses; fragments of the Parthenon frieze, busts of the Greek dramatists and philosophers; copies of Greek plates and amphorae; and in the centre of the room, on a round black-grained marble pedestal, a bust of Homer. This was the room, the great

53

magnificent room for Thomas.

'I feel like Lord Carnarvon opening the tomb of King Tut,' said Thomas.

'Like a lord, eh,' she said. 'Well, for what it may be worth to you, consider yourself lord of the manor; it's yours. And there's more...'

She took him through two large glass doors hidden by the main stairway. It was a children's theatre, a perfect theatre; it was all there; long wooden forms to seat six hundred children; a stage with deep red and gold curtains which opened and closed; tin containers for footlights and toplights; and behind stage, rolls of scenery; even a thunder sheet.

'I shall have to get permission – '

'No need to get permission, Mr Davies; permission to bring children as part of their school timetable was granted when Mr Horsfall began his people's palace.'

'And nobody has ever...?'

'Never ever.'

Thomas was so excited that he got on his bike without putting on his clips, and caught his trouser bottoms in the chain. He had discovered Knossos, Mycenae and Troy; he had been admitted to Olympus. And the theatre! The theatre was icing on the cake! He remembered the audiences when he'd been with Dick, Charlie and Miss Cowgill on Saturday nights; different audiences, different entertainment, but hundreds of happy faces; he'd get the kids to teach each other by entertainment. The glory that was Greece in the squalor that was Ancoats!

There was commotion in the headmaster's office when Thomas arrived. A joiner was singing 'The Spinning Wheel Song' in a low crooning voice as he puttied in a new sheet of glass. Dick, Charlie and Miss Cowgill, like hens pecking for corn, were picking up broken glass which had been shattered and scattered everywhere.

'They broke in over the weekend,' said Dick. 'They've stolen the blooming old gramophone.'

'The police?' asked Thomas by way of suggestion.

'Ar, sure we'll not be troubling the likes of those fine gentlemen, we'll not at all. For whosoever ran away with the gramophone needs the money more than we need the music. Would ye put a man behind bars for stealing "The British Grenadiers" now? And his darling wife having to go begging on the parish or into the workhouse? And his fine young children put in a home maybe? Ar, sure we'll let it be!'

'Besides,' said Charlie, 'Miss Cowgill has kindly volunteered to play the scholars in on the piano to melodies sweetly played in tune.'

'Selections from Gilbert and Sullivan,' she smiled. She looked proud and happy as though she had waved her knitting needle like a magic wand and caused the gramophone to disappear. She bounced to the window and looked the joiner straight in the face:

The flowers that bloom in the spring tra-la
    Bring promise of merry sunshine.

The surprised joiner touched his cap to her and slowly vanished from the window.


There was an eerie atmosphere in the school. It put a damper on Thomas's enthusiasm for his inaugural visit to the museum. It was a something, a vibrating something in the air which he couldn't understand. It was like waiting on a heavy day for a thunderstorm. The boys were quiet, well behaved, subdued; there was no fidgeting, no giggling, no passing of notes; they answered his questions; they didn't laugh at his jokes.

'Calm before the storm,' said Dick Wilson at playtime over the tea and arrowroot biscuit.

'What storm? What's it all about?'

'Welcome to your gory bed, or to victory!'

'You're talking in riddles, both of you.'

Miss Cowgill stared into her empty teacup as though reading the tea-leaves.

'There's going to be a big gang fight tonight,' said Dick. 'Oh, heaven knows what it's over; it doesn't matter. Maybe somebody kicked somebody else's dog; maybe the Italian kids saw one of their girls with one of the Irish kids. But there'll be blood on the streets tonight.'

'Can't we do something to stop it?'

'Ach, they'd cut ye up into thin slices like boiled ham at a funeral if ye tried. They'll make sure none of us are around when

55

it starts. We'll be escorted out of Ancoats. The streets will be cleared; there'll be no authority of any description to witness the shinanikins; people will stay in their homes. At about six of the clock the streets will be empty, even the cats and dogs will have cleared off. Half an hour later a couple of hundred kids will be kicking, screaming, swearing, yelling, biting, banging, thumping and belting the living daylights out of each other the likes ye'd never have seen. I'm closing the school for the rest of the day.' Dick offered his whiskey bottle, but nobody wanted any. 'Maybe ye'd best be away to your tram, Miss Cowgill, for I'm thinking they'll not be in the mood for one of your pretty little cuckoo songs yet awhile. I'm sure Mr Macgregor will be delighted to accompany ye.'

Miss Cowgill put on her hat and coat. 'Then heigh-ho the holly! This life is most jolly!' she said as they left the office.

Dick Wilson was met by six senior boys; they walked with him to his tram stop and waited till the tram rattled along. Six more boys ran alongside Thomas's bicycle until they reached the Pin Mill Brow boundary. Throughout the run they gasped nothing but courtesies; admiring his sturdy bicycle, praising his balance on it, saying how much they'd enjoyed his last lesson, even volunteering history dates like the murder of Thomas à Becket and the execution of King Charles. They waved and wished him a very good night as he freewheeled down the cobbled slope towards the Medlock bridge.

It was one of the most hideous street fights Ancoats had ever pretended not to know about. In the middle of the knees, blood, boots and knives, half a dozen Italian kids grabbed hold of Kelly and dragged him over the cobbles to an entryway.

'Was it you put your finger up the little Maria, eh?' said Moroni. 'So we cut the finger off. Hold him! Who got the sharpest knife?'

'No, please! For the love of Jesus! It wasn't me!' screamed Kelly. 'I told him not to do it! God's honour I did! 'Twas Keenan!'

They ran away from him in search of Keenan. Kelly lay dead with a knife in his back.

Keenan was whirling a bicycle chain around like an autogyro.

One of the Italians dived for his legs and brought him down. The rest tumbled on top of him.

'Cut his bloody finger off!' was yelled by several of the boys. Most of the Irish and Italian kids stopped fighting each other and grouped around to watch a boy having his finger cut off. There was silence except for Keenan's shouting for mercy. He kicked and punched and wriggled and squirmed. There was a sudden gasp from his attackers. A knife had accidentally slashed his eye open. Keenan screamed like a girl.

A few hundred lads ran away in many directions, and the street was soon empty except for Keenan screaming as his hands clawed at a bloodstained patch of cobbles, and across the street the still figure of his pal.

> Summer is a-coming in,
>    Loud sings the cuckoo!

A third of the class simply sang 'cuckoo, cuckoo' throughout the song.

> Groweth seed and bloweth mead,
>    And springs the wood anew,
>       Sing cuckoo!

Thomas couldn't believe his ears the next morning. He was compelled to rush into the hall. Miss Cowgill was blissfully waving her knitting needle, happy and contented. Some of the boys had their arms in slings, leg bandages, and patches over their eyes. But there was a peaceful atmosphere of relief and relaxation. The boys enjoyed their cuckoo song. Thomas rushed into the office.

'How could she? How could they? How could we?' he shouted at Dick. 'A boy was murdered! Another lost an eye! Our boys! Our boys!'

'Accidental death,' corrected Dick. 'There's no such thing as a murder in Ancoats; there's just an awful lot of accidental deaths.'

'What are we going to do about it, Dick?'

'Every boy will bring threepence towards the lad's burial. Remember this, me fine young feller me lad, that when children die before their parents, then, for the sake of the parents if nothing else, that youngster will be given the grandest of funerals, something for the parents to remember. The lad who's lost an eye will be in the Royal Eye Hospital for many weeks. Perhaps ye could drop a poetry book in for him on your way home. He'll still be able to read with one eye.'

For the first time, Thomas felt that Dick was callous.

'We've got to stop it, Dick!' he yelled, banging his fist down on Dick's desk. 'We've got to do something to stop it!'

'Hey, there, steady on, me young fighting cock, don't get your feathers rustled,' said Dick. He handed Thomas the whiskey bottle, and Thomas took a swig. 'We're doing the hell of a lot. Would ye imagine now that there was no Raglan Street School, and that there was no need for Thomas Davies, Charles Macgregor, Miss Cowgill and Richard Wilson to get out of their warm beds every morning to come here and dole out free milk? Sure the little sods would be roaming the streets like packs o' wolves; and how many more accidental deaths d'ye think there'd be then, eh? Put that in your pipe and smoke it!'

Thomas marched his first class, with its average number of wounded, down the street to the Horsfall Museum. Miss Hindshaw smiled at them as they filed in. Their eyes opened wide as they stared at the statues in the Athens Room; they'd never seen such nakedness. Each boy was afraid of coughing in case the coughing drew attention to himself.

'Well, what does anybody think? Haynes?'

'They're dead dirty, sir.'

'Moroni?'

'Yeah, mucky, sir. They're showing all their things.'

'They're gods and goddesses,' said Thomas.

'Then they should know better than to show their things,' said Frascatti. 'The bloody police would have you.'

'Our God has a towel round him if nowt else,' said Haynes. 'And that's decent and holy.'

'They were Greek gods thousands of years before Christ,' continued Thomas.

'That explains it then, sir,' said Haynes. 'They had to pawn their clothes when Jesus came and put them out of work.'

'This is called mythology. It isn't true.'

'Then are you stuffing our heads with a pack of lies, sir? Only we're not supposed to deal in lies, like you told us Ruddy Hard Kipper said.'

There was a laugh.

'Please, sir, is all that about Jesus a pack of lies as well?'

Thomas cleared his throat. 'The ancient Greeks believed in a beautiful mind in a beautiful body. They saw no shame in the human body. Now I can march you right back to school and ask Mr Macgregor to drill you and make you do exercises until you develop beautiful bodies. Or you can stay here, keep quiet, and learn to develop beautiful minds. Which is it to be?'

'We'd rather have beautiful minds, sir.'


A dozen lads dragged Moroni down on the wet tiles of the urinal. He'd been caught playing with himself in the urinal, and he'd said it was because he was thinking of the goddess statue with no arms and big tits.

'Then you must learn to develop a beautiful mind,' said one of the gang. They pulled his trousers down and it was suggested they should pee one by one on his stomach; but it was nearly whistle time so they took turns to spit on his belly instead. The whistle blew.

'What do you think of Mavis?' Frascatti asked Maguire. 'Him and his statues and that?'

'Me dad says he's an all-time loser. And he's come to our school because he thinks we're the lowest of the low, and that makes him feel the biggest of the big. Y'know, like Zeus.'

'You mean Apollo. Zeus was the one with the beard. Apollo was the one what drove the sun like a milk cart.'

'Hurry up, you two!' shouted Charlie Macgregor.

# The parson owned his skill

The message monitor brought a note to Thomas's classroom to say that Mr Wilson wished to see him in his office immediately. When he looked in he saw two serious clergymen seated bolt upright with their arms folded.

'Ar, now, come in, Mr Davies, will ye,' said Dick Wilson. ' 'Tis an honour to be introducing ye to the Reverend Watkins of the Church of England and Father O'Brien of the Catholic Church. Sure I believe they've a little matter they wish to be discussing with ye, Mr Davies.'

Dick begun writing on a sheet of foolscap paper. 'I'll be taking the words down if there's no objection?' There was no objection.

Father O'Brien began: 'Because the law of England insists that if there is no room in the Catholic school, some children must be sent to other schools like this one – '

'And indeed,' chipped in the Reverend Watkins, 'many of my parishioners have to send their children to this … er … municipal school. So we're presenting ourselves together, united as it were, to demand that you resign from this school immediately, or that your headmaster here discharges you.'

'Well, I'm gratified that my sin, whatever it is, has brought about some form of church unity,' said Thomas. 'However, might I ask what it is that upsets you?'

'Ye've filled their blithering heads with blasphemy, that's what ye've done,' shouted Father O'Brien. 'Ye've introduced them to heathenish gods and graven images, so ye have.'

'I've taught them mythology.'

'Is that what you call it?' said Reverend Watkins. 'You've hinted at the most indecent things concerning Our Lord Jesus Christ. Things I would never have heard about had it not been for the good Father O'Brien telling me some of the evil notions his boys had told him in confession.'

'They've said them, not I,' said Thomas. 'But they're my scholars, and I'll take responsibility.'

'Ye've displayed naked women to their innocent eyes.'

'Is nakedness a sin?'

'Indeed it is,' said the Reverend Watkins. 'Did not Adam and Eve have to cover up their nakedness?'

'From what I gather,' said Thomas, 'most of their innocent eyes have already seen the naked female body through keyholes. Many of them have to share a room or even a bed with their sisters.'

'There's enough evil in Ancoats!' shouted Father O'Brien.

'I couldn't agree with you more. Some nights ago there was a most appalling street fight, but I'm pleased to see neither of you gentlemen were injured trying to stop it. I'm sure you both did your best to prevent the violence.'

'That's enough!' shouted the priest. 'We're wasting time and words! We demand your resignation. You're not fit to be in charge of greyhound kennels!'

'If Mr Davies chooses to resign,' smiled Dick Wilson, 'that's his business. But I have no intention of discharging him, he's a first-class schoolmaster. When he started here, Raglan Street was a waiting depot for the magistrates' courts. It hasn't changed much, but today it's beginning, so as you'd hardly notice it, to look just a wee bit like an educational centre.'

'It makes no difference what you think,' said the Reverend Watkins, tapping the foolscap paper Dick Wilson was writing on. 'When the Education Committee gets that report they'll take all the action necessary. They'll have to take notice of two clergymen.'

'The Education Committee?' smiled Dick Wilson innocently. 'This isn't for the Education Committee. I'm sorry; I should have told ye; though ye didn't object when I asked you. This is to send to one of those newspapers which likes publishing this kind of article. Ar, sure ye know how daft some newspapers are; anything to create a stir.'

The two clergymen looked into each other's eyes for a few seconds as though communicating by telepathy. The priest coughed.

'Indeed now, and didn't Our Lord preach forgiveness? To turn the other cheek?'

'We just came to talk things over,' endorsed Reverend Watkins.

61

'Indeed we did. We did indeed.'

'We are prepared to forgive the schoolmaster's error of judgement,' summed up the Church of England's minister, 'and are sure he will give us no further cause for complaint.'

Thomas was about to reply in a blunt aggressive way, but Dick Wilson beat him to it.

'Rest assured, gentlemen, Mr Davies will continue to teach the histories of the ancient civilisations, and I shall watch him very carefully. Thank you for your kind concern, and the interest you have taken in our school.' The two gentlemen left the office.

'Ye'll be getting to know them quite well in the future to my way of thinking,' said Dick, pouring himself out a drink,

'Thanks.'

'Ar, sure not at all. But tell me, me fine young feller, is it true? Is the blooming place full of naked statues?'

'There's Aphrodite – '

'Is there now? Aphrodite, eh? Aphrodite without a nightie! D'y'know, there's a comic song there. 'Tis the sort of thing would amuse Paddy Reilly if he went to a museum. Sure I'll have to work it in. Ye're a good feller, Thomas, ye are that!'


'There you are now, Thomas, a nice duck egg. There's more iron in a duck egg than the ordinary ones,' said his mother. 'And I thought it would make a nice change from porridge.'

Thomas cracked the top off his boiled egg. His mother stopped half-way through pouring out his cup of tea. 'Since they knocked the head off Jesus, Moss Side has gone downhill and downhill,' she sighed.

'Then why do we live here?' he asked. 'We could easily get a little house across the Mersey.'

'They think they're somebodies out there.'

'Well, we're somebodies.'

'Oh no we're not. They'd soon find out my son was teaching in Ancoats. I wouldn't be able to hold my head up. Besides, as I've said before, this was your dad's house, and he wouldn't want us to leave it.'

Thomas took a quick glance at the picture of the young officer on the wall. His dad's house! That, as he well knew, was the end of the argument. Duck eggs and sticky porridge. He bet his dad breathed a sigh of relief when he found himself spinning down in a smoking Bristol Bulldog, no more duck eggs, no more porridge. He had to protect himself with humour inside his quiet brain during the daily breakfast scenes. He was embarrassed.

Dick Wilson and Charlie Macgregor were continually inviting him to spend Saturday nights with them at the clubs or at the stadiums. He accepted their hospitality; a meal or a few drinks; but how could he ever invite them back to his house in Moss Side, his dad's house, his mother's house? A decaying terraced house in a dismal district. If his mother didn't like them, she would go up to her room and stay there; she didn't like many people. She had done this when he had brought his student colleagues home from the university. When he mentioned it to her afterwards, she would say, 'A body gets tired. Could I help it if I needed to lay my head down on the pillow?' He dare not tell her where he went on Saturday nights; imagine him saying that his headmaster was a comedian in workingmen's clubs, that Mr Macgregor was an all-in wrestler at the spit and sawdust stadiums! He told her he went to a debating society.

When he had hinted, just gently and discreetly hinted, that perhaps he could find digs, with the promise to visit her often, she had replied: 'Oh, yes, if you think you can do better somewhere else, don't let me stand in your path. Of course, I might as well put my head in the gas oven without you.'

He would have loved a flat, one like Charlie Macgregor, near the river. Only a few Sundays ago he had met Charlie after the Terriers parade and they had gone back to his flat for a few bottles of beer. Afterwards, cold though it was, they had taken a rowing boat out on the river. Charlie had done all the rowing, and had sung at the top of his voice:

Sing me a song of a lad that is gone,
    Say could that lad be I?
Merry of soul he sailed on a day
    Over the sea to Skye.

'There ye are, laddie, this isn't the Clyde, but if I row on for another thirty miles we'll come to Liverpool and maybe we can stop there and build ships.'

'If you like. It'd make a change.'

'My father built ships, y'know. Worked for John Brown's at Clydebank. He built the *Lusitania*.'

'On his own?'

'Och no, there were a few thousand others passing him things. Then he got killed in the war.'

'Sorry.'

'Hero he was. Though there's some say he was an idiot. Got a medal posthumously. It was at Gallipoli. They'd beached the ship ready for the soldiers to scramble ashore, but there were too many Turks with too many bullets. They were ordered to abandon the ship and get on to another one alongside. But my father refused. Apparently he pointed to one of those iron crests which said "John Brown. Clydebank" and told them he'd built the ship and wasn't going to let the Turks have it. He'd built his own tomb and cenotaph in John Brown's yard. Then my mother took me and we moved in with an insurance man. I was doing all right because I'd passed to Edinburgh and was reading medicine. Me, a doctor, eh, laddie? And then one New Year's Eve – aye, Hogmanay – my mother supped a full bottle of scotch and jumped off a bridge near Saint Patrick's into the Clyde. She was washed up near Dumbarton.'

'Christ, Charlie!'

'I was in love with a girl who comforted me – Jeannie; Jeannie with the light brown hair if you like – and I carried on cutting up rats. I met her in Glasgow every weekend and we'd cycle – aye, laddie, I had an old pushbike like yours – up to Loch Lomond, and we'd go out on the steamer and talk of emigrating to Canada when I was a fully fledged doctor. She died of pneumonia. And I caught the next train down to the land of the Sassenachs, and I've never been back to Scotland since.' He tapped his forehead. 'Scotland is only in the mind, and it's a Scotland that never was, and never will be. Even that kilt I wear for the wrestling is just a random mixture of bright colours, no clan would ever own it. And now, Thomas, I'm mindful that we've a couple of bottles of beer still unscrewed back in the flat, so let's row for the bank.'

Thomas's excuse to his mother for Sunday was that he had been to a special schoolteachers' service in the cathedral; she could hardly condemn him for that. She complained enough about loneliness as it was; heaven knows what she'd have said if he'd told her he'd been supping beer in an easy chair and looking out over the trees to the river. He'd suggested she got a dog to keep her company, but she said it would mess on the floor, so he suggested a wireless set, which wouldn't mess on the floor.

'That would be nice, Thomas; then you and I can sit and listen to music hall on Saturday nights instead of you going out debating.'

Thomas only felt free and strong when he was involved with his school, and happily he became more and more involved as the days went by.

The boys had spent weeks getting the children's theatre ready for the first rehearsals. They'd volunteered to scrub the wooden planking of the theatre floor and the stage. They'd learned how to wire footlights and toplights in both series and parallel. They'd stitched the decaying rolls of canvas scenery, patching some of it with cleaned and starched coal bags. He had shown them how to paint winding lanes diminishing into perspective over undulating hills; how to paint trees and hedgerows and distant cottages. Tins of paint, new brushes, wooden planks for furniture, even coloured electric light bulbs seemed to come from nowhere; they were brought by the boys. Thomas had been advised by Dick Wilson never to ask from whence they came.

'For did the ancient Hebrews question the loaves and fishes?' he asked. 'Did they expect an invoice for the manna from heaven? They did not! They got stuck in with their knives and forks, and chalked it all up to a miracle.'

The lights lit up without fusing; the curtains parted and came together again smoothly and noiselessly; the scenery rolled down evenly on its pulley ropes; the thunder sheet sounded like real thunder. Thomas's next task was to interest the boys in play-acting. Play-acting, to their way of thinking, was what little girls did in the street; they played at mothers and sweethearts and nurses, and sometimes a wolf came from Devonshire or a farmer wanted a wife. He took them into the Athens Room, showed them a photograph of a Greek open air theatre, and told them of a man named Aeschylus who composed the first ever drama.

'He must have been a big soft girl, sir,' said Saar.

Thomas gave them a vivid description of the battle of Salamis and the battle of Marathon. He told them that Aeschylus had fought at both. They no doubt visualised Aeschylus as wiping the blood off his sword on his sleeve, washing the blood from his hands, then sitting down to write a play in copperplate writing; but Thomas didn't mind this blood and thunder approach; they were hearing about Aeschylus.

'And let me tell you something more about him,' he went on. 'After the Greeks had thoroughly defeated the Persians, he was asked to produce a play to celebrate victory. It was called *The Persians* – and was it going cockadoodle-doo with glory? It was not. It dealt with the sorrows of the losers. He killed Persians in battle; he felt sorry for them in defeat. Big soft girl, Saar?'

'No, sir,'

'Good. I'll tell you about Goethe some day. Ever heard of Goethe, Saar?'

'No, sir.'

'He fought against the French revolutionary army in 1792. He was also a poet. He was also a German. I believe you know what a German is?'

'Yes, sir. I'm one.'

The first group of plays he decided to present were medieval pageant plays; he considered they were tough enough and simple enough for his boys. It was also the earliest form of English drama; and anyway Christmas wasn't far off, so what better than a nativity play or two. He read the first one out to them, and there were questions.

'Please, sir, that bit where them shepherds is arguing the toss about being taxed and shamed and hand-tamed by the gentry, wasn't they in a union or owt?'

'The pageant plays were put on by trades guilds,' explained Thomas. 'They had no unions as such to voice their complaints.'

'Then could us shepherds carry banners asking for more money?'

'Yes, I suppose you could.'

'Please, sir, could I be Mac? He's got the best part cos he steals the sheep and that's better than begging the bosses for more money. Me dad says God helps them what helps themselves.'

'Is the sheep supposed to be the infant Jesus?'

'No. This is just a general knock-about before the shepherds toss Mac in a blanket. Then the shepherds go to Bethlehem. It says here "the shepherds arrive at Bethlehem."'

'How do they do that, sir, if they're in England?'

'They bloody swim,' said a voice.

'No they bloody don't,' added another. 'They join the Palestine Police and get sent over. Me uncle did.'

'That's an idea, sir. Can we have comic policemen chasing Mac, like the Keystone Cops?'

'There are no policemen,' said Thomas. 'Only angels.'

'Well, comic angels, sir. I don't mind being an angel if I can get to use me fists.'

'Sir, why go all the way to Bethlehem for a stable? We've got dozens of a railway stables under the arches in Great Ancoats Street. Couldn't Jesus have been born in a stable in Ancoats?'

'I suppose he could.'

'That'll be better then, sir, cos we've got the trains shunting all the time and it'll sound more real.'

'Trouble is, sir, there's no shepherds in Ancoats cos there's no sheep.'

'There's sheep's heads. We had one for tea last night. And me dad had the brains.'

'It'd be an improvement on the ones he's got.'

'I'll smash your bloody face in, Maguire.'

'We can't have shepherds, sir. Most of our dads work in cotton, when there's work. Cotton workers, sir? Workers what want money for bread.'

Thomas listened to the conversations with delight; it was like something from *A Midsummer Night's Dream*; it was medieval, blunt and simple. He accepted that the stable would be under the railway arches of Ancoats; that the shepherds would be disgruntled cotton workers. There were more blunt and simple views after he read the second nativity play.

'Why did Joseph threaten to thump Mary?'

'Cos she said she was having a kid, and he knew it wasn't his. But the angel put him right.'

'Perhaps the angel was really the lodger pretending to be an angel, and it was his kid.'

'I wouldn't blame her fancying the lodger. Joseph was a nasty old sod. Look how nasty he got when the angel woke him up in the middle of the night.'

'That's cos he's an old man. I bet your dad would half kill you if you woke him in the middle of the night.'

'I wouldn't need to wake him, he gets up enough times when he's been on the beer. Me mam shouts to him to be quiet about it

67

cos all the world can hear him peeing into the tin po.'

'Aye, but it wasn't for a piss though, was it? The angel told him to put his keks on and find a donkey and bugger off to Egypt from Herod.'

'Ah, but he tried to wriggle out of it by saying he didn't know the way to Egypt. I bet you wouldn't know the way to Egypt from Great Ancoats Street, not if you was asked.'

'No, but the donkey would.'

'Give over! Never trust a flaming donkey! Egypt? You'd end up on on Blackpool sands; that's where they all go.'

'Hee-haw! Hee-haw! Mike Moroni has big ears!'

It was intended that those not playing character parts would form a choir to sing the ancient yule-tide carols, but there was an objection that they were being turned into cissie choirboys. It was finally agreed that they could be Robin Hood's merry men of Sherwood with bows and arrows in their hands. Those who couldn't make bows and arrows would bring their catapults.

It was decided that coal sacks would be used for costumes, but they all wanted to wear their Sunday Jackie Coogan caps, for Jackie Coogan caps were all the rage. However, Thomas insisted that the good characters wore the peaks at the back of the head, the bad ones over one ear, the angels, or outlaws, as they now were, dead square to the front military fashion. The boy who was Joseph said he'd wear his father's bowler hat, it would be a good fit if he packed the brim with newspapers, and his dad wouldn't mind, for his dad always said a bowler hat was the relic of old decency.

Thomas was pleased. He could see the possibilities for the children's theatre. The amber lights brought sunshine to the stage, even if the streets outside were brown with fog; the painted hills invited adventure, the twisting narrowing pathway pointed to an horizon beyond the mills. Their silly talk, crude and blasphemous, had shown enthusiasm and imagination. His boys had only seen painted hills; they'd only heard talk of sea and sand; they'd never been anywhere near an angel or Bethlehem or Athens; he was building a Parthenon in their minds. His lice-ridden barbarians were beginning to ask questions.

Thomas glanced through Dick Wilson's *Manchester Evening*

*News* before putting on his cycle clips. Miss Cowgill was leading her last song:

> The sunlight now is streaming
>   Through all the valley bright,
> And pearling brooks are gleaming
>   And flashing in the light.

Then his eye caught an advertisement in the paper. Pauldens, the department store in All Saints, wanted a man with artistic ability to work on Saturdays only.

School was closing early because thick fog was coming down, but he was determined to get to Pauldens. As though sent by the angels, a tram car came along with its destination lit up, 'All Saints'. Although most other vehicles were coming to a stand-still, the tram, being on lines, would get through; and he cycled behind the tram in the middle of the lines, stopping when it stopped, starting when it started.

The job was to cut out and paint figures for window and counter displays.

'Experience?' asked Mr Wingate, the manager.

'I've painted scenery for the theatre,' he replied, which wasn't altogether a lie.

'Can you do winking bunny rabbits for gardening? Chuckling chickens for the poultry counter? Happy little piggy-wigs for sausages?'

'Yes, sir.'

'Cunning crocodiles snapping at handbag bargains? Clever little squirrels storing up enamel pots and pans for winter? Wise old owls in mortarboards and gowns for back to school? Rampant lions for Buy British?'

'Yes, sir.'

'You're the only one who's been able to get here because of the fog, so the job's yours. Your first job on Saturday will be to construct an Aladdin's Cave, with fairies, mushrooms, woodcutters, gnomes, goblins, pixies and Red Riding Hood for Father Christmas, and a sign glittering with gilt to read "Christmas Parcels. One Shilling. Form a Queue."'

Thomas was so excited as he pushed his bike home that he didn't remember how he'd managed it through the fog; he crossed roads and turned corners instinctively. He would miss his Saturday nights with Paddy Reilly, Rob Roy and, occasionally, Miss Cowgill, but he was one of them now; he was a Saturday man. No more lies to his mother; no more debating societies and cathedral services; what's more, no chance of him having to listen to music hall on the wireless. He would be earning money with his own sideline; enough money to insist he paid his mother something for his keep; the start of independence. He might find a girl who would go to the pictures with him.

'I'm glad you've got a real job at last,' said his mother, putting a plate of steaming potato cakes under his nose. 'Eat them while they're hot.'

'It's only a part-time job; Saturdays only, nine till nine,' he told her. 'My real job is schoolmaster.'

'Nonsense,' she said. 'Being a schoolmaster in Ancoats isn't a real job as anybody can tell you. But working in a department store is.'

'What? Painting a smile on the face of a duck?'

'You never know where it can lead.'


Thomas learned to tell the seasons in Ancoats. In summer, people sat on their steps and children played in the street; the air was heavy and stank of rubber and sulphur; each house in each street had a linnet in a tiny box cage nailed up on the outside wall near the door. The only migration of these sad linnets when winter came would be to the middens.

Autumn came with dampness and fireworks. Fireworks exploded everywhere at all times; they were sometimes pushed through letterboxes, and the fire engine bell rang often. It was also the season when funerals began, usually for the very young and the very old; his boys were old enough to survive; just occasionally, and only occasionally, would he get an illiterate note to ask if a boy's name could be taken off the register because he had been taken. Short of accidental deaths, his boys would live.

Christmas began in Ancoats two weeks before anywhere else. The ceiling of every parlour was thickly festooned with red, white, blue, yellow and green paper chains and decorations, not just from corners to centre but from sides to centre as well. In the centre of the parlour was the gas globe, and Thomas was surprised not to hear fire engine bells, until he found out that people lived in their sculleries over Christmas and the parlour was only used on Christmas Day. Unlike the dwellings, the churches, schools and beerhouses had electric lights and the electric globes were covered in red hangings. His district of Moss Side had fewer streamers than Ancoats, and at times when he cycled to Northenden he noticed that the posher the districts became the fewer the decorations. The kids sang carols in the street, the Protestant kids sang 'We Three Kings' and 'Away In A Manger', and the Catholic kids sang 'See Amid The Winter's Snow', and there were sometimes minor street fights over the different carols.

It was a busy Christmas approach for Thomas. He worked hard on his Christmas grotto, which would be for the children of the middle classes whose parents could afford the tram fare and a shilling for a parcel. He was proud of himself; the grotto was enchanting; he had created magic. Father Christmas sat on a throne; on his right hand was the fairy queen who took the shillings and handed out the parcels; at the back of the display, beyond reach of the children, a grandmother relaxed in a four poster bed; she had nothing to do except change the gramophone record on a turntable from the jolly dances of 'The Nutcracker Suite' to 'Jingle Bells'. There was a frequent change of grandmothers because girls who told Mr Wingate that it was their time for being unwell were given an hour to relax on the bed in the grotto.

He worked hard on week nights with the rehearsals of the pageant plays; he had to research and rewrite the original texts to bring them up to date.

But his main task during the day was to teach the Christmas school leavers how to write applications for jobs and how to behave at interviews; his own recent experience with Pauldens had not only given him an insight into job interviews but confidence in giving the right short sharp answers to get the job.

'And the correct answer to every question is "Yes, sir",' he told them. 'Working on the children's theatre has taught a lot of you to saw wood, wire lights and mix paint; others have acquired the ability to open your mouths and speak on a stage. If they ask you if you've had experience, say "Yes, sir". I want you lot to get good jobs, not sweeping up and brewing tea and cleaning windows, but

71

good jobs; jobs which will allow you to wear the emblems of success.'

'What are them, sir?'

'A fountain pen in the top pocket, a wristlet watch on the wrist, a wallet in the inside pocket.'

'What's the good of a wallet if you've no money to put in it, sir?'

'With a wristlet watch to keep yourselves punctual, and a pen to do your best writing with, you'll soon earn something to put in your wallet.' Unfortunately he didn't possess a wristlet watch to demonstrate with. Every afternoon he borrowed Dick Wilson's *Evening News* and wrote job vacancies on the blackboard. There was an office boy's job going at Fairey Aviation.

'But, sir,' said Alker, 'as soon as we write Ancoats on our addresses they'll wipe their bums on the letter.'

'That all depends on how you write "Ancoats",' said Thomas, and he wrote the word in his most magnificent handwriting on the board. The A had a flawlessly curved upstroke, the downstroke was thick and straight, the crossing of the A was a swanky flourished curve; the t was crossed with a long upward pointing sweep.

'There,' he said, standing back and admiring his own work; 'write Ancoats good, and it'll look good. Write it good enough times and people will begin to believe you.' A thought came to him. 'Is this a good school?' he asked.

'It's better than the reformatory!' somebody shouted.

'I'll ask again. Is this a good school?'

'Yes!' shouted the class.

'Good!' he smiled. 'Well, most other good schools, like Eton and Harrow – '

'What part of Ancoats are they in, sir?' asked Haynes.

'Most other good schools,' he continued, ignoring the remark, 'were founded by famous men hundreds of years ago. Now, what's the name of this school?'

'Raglan Street!'

'Very clever of you to remember, Shaughnessy. Now all the streets in this part of Ancoats are named after important lords of the last century. Palmerston Street is the best example. And Raglan Street is called after Lord Raglan. Who was he? Well, Lord Raglan was said to be responsible for the charge of the Light Brigade at Balaclava in the Crimean War of 1854.' He rushed to the cupboard, brought out a Tennyson, thumbed to the right page quickly, and read out the poem in a vivid and exciting way.

'So there,' he said when he'd finished. 'I've given the school a tradition which I expect you all to live up to.'

'But they was all wiped out, sir. They were bloody losers!'

'Aye, and so are we,' said Shaughnessy.

'More than half returned. More than half survived,' said Thomas. He printed 'Charge For The Guns' at the top of the blackboard. 'That will be our school motto from now on. It will stay up on the blackboard. There's not going to be another war, so the word "gun" is metaphorical. The job going at Fairey Aviation is a gun. Charge for it! All good jobs are guns. Charge for them! Some of you will be successful.' He then wrote 'Dear Sir' on the board and wrote out a letter of application for them to copy.

About a week later, Thomas's bike was rattling over the cobbles on his way home when a yellow glint between two cobbles took his eye. He squeezed the brakes. It was a gold wristlet watch. He looked around; the street was empty. But a gold watch in Ancoats was impossible; absolutely impossible; nobody would ever dare come into the district wearing such a valuable watch. And even supposing somebody had dropped it, the hawk eyes of a dozen hungry men would have seen it and snatched it before it hit the cobbles. But it was there, it was a gold watch, it was keeping time, it was ticking. Just an ordinary watch was something he'd always wanted but never been able to afford, but a gold watch! He put it in his pocket and cycled away at twice his normal speed. He wanted to keep it. He knew he couldn't keep it. He cycled to police headquarters in the city and handed it in. They took his name and address and told him if it wasn't claimed it was his. He hoped and hoped it would never be claimed; he knew it would be. Who would not report the loss of a solid gold watch?

# Full well they laughed

The tickets were free, and the theatre was packed to standing with over six hundred snotty-nosed baggy-arsed dirty-faced children. Thomas peeped through a specially made hole in the curtain as they fought their way. He saw Dick and his wife, Charlie and a young woman, and Miss Cowgill sitting on fold-up chairs at the back, also the two local clergymen; also a reporter from the *Evening News* and one from the *Evening Chronicle*. It was wild, noisy, rowdy, happy; it was as he'd hoped it would be. He was more than a little worried about the crib, this had been constructed by his boys, and he'd only seen it for the first time minutes before the audience came in.

It was a stable, and it was realistic; of that there was no doubt. It was filled with horse harnesses and reins and nosebags; there was a large amount of straw, and, he suspected, horse manure. There was even a sign above the cradle in the centre of the stage which said 'Trespassers Will Be Prosecuted. Property of The London and North Eastern Railway'. For a second, Thomas had a sickening worry that his boys might have stolen a horse as well.

His boys, unknown to him, had also changed some of the action and composed some of their own lavatory wall rhyming couplets, as when Robin Hood stepped forward to start the pageant and drew his bow and arrow around the audience.

If you make this play a farce,
  You'll get an arrow up your arse,
So bloody keep quiet and sit dead tight
  Or you'll end up in a fight.

It was imaginative, it had a touch of flair, it was vulgar. Miss Hindshaw, who had been standing at the exit with her arms folded, disappeared with her hand to her mouth. She returned five minutes later.

Then the shepherds or, as they were, the Chartists marched

on to a song Thomas had discovered:

In eighteen hundred and forty-two
    When I was just a lad,
I worked for next to nothing
    And the hours were very bad,
So I became a Chartist
    And decided I would strike,
And off I went to Manchester
    With a broomstick for a pike.

There was a shout from Dick Wilson way at the back of the theatre. 'Come on, kids, give 'em a hand!'
'With a broomstick for a pike!' yelled six hundred children.

If anyone tried to stop us
    We punched 'em in the lugs,
And closed the other factories
    By stealing the boiler plugs.
Dragoons were set upon us,
    Artillery was employed,
But we marched on up to Gould Street
    And the gasworks was destroyed.

'The gasworks was destroyed!' shouted the six hundred. There followed a battle between the Chartists and Robin Hood's merry outlaws. The kids jumped up and down in their seats. And then there was a thunder roll from the thunder sheet; the amber lights changed to blue; a spotlight fell on to the cradle, which was just a box stencilled 'Sankey's Soaps'. Robin Hood's men sang 'Away In A Manger' in their best Miss Cowgill voices. Thomas couldn't believe the transformation. From rough roister-doistering, the atmosphere changed to religious serenity. Some of the boys in the audience wiped their eyes with the sleeves of their coats; most of the girls lifted the hems of their frocks to dab at tears. Tears streamed down Thomas's eyes. It was the medieval touch; it was working as it must have worked five hundred years ago. Jesus stood up in his box; and Jesus, who was Sean Flaherty, added lines of his own:

75

Praise be to God and peace on earth;
    Pay the working man what he's worth.

Thomas noticed the two clergymen leave the theatre.

So much for the Wakefield play; the Coventry one which followed was even rowdier, with moments even more religious. The main theme was Herod's ordering his soldiers to slaughter the babies: for this the stage was flooded with red lights, and many children bit their fingernails.

The women in the play wore coal sacks over their heads for shawls; they carried simple rag dolls for babies; for distant gunfire the thunder sheet was used again. The fight began when the soldiers marched in to kill the babies. It was obvious by the thuds that the rag dolls had stones or half-bricks in their heads; the women used their dolls to slosh the soldiers with. There was a time when it looked as if the women might win, but the wooden swords of Herod's soldiers had a longer reach than waved dolls, and the women fell back. Robin Hood's merry men tried to rescue them, but they had no arrows left. Instead, they marched down the theatre aisle:

For they'd have slaughtered all of us,
    Our children and our wives,
Because we had a charter for
    A chance to better lives.
We felt we were defeated,
    And our spirits fell so low,
When the Chartist men retreated
    From the Battle of Granby Row.

The red stage became a blue stage. The white spotlight circled on the stage, at first accidentally illuminating the 'Trespassers Will be Prosecuted' sign, then coming correctly to rest on the soap box cradle, although there was no infant Jesus in it because Flaherty was also taking the part of Herod. The merry men sang 'Silent Night' softly and sweetly; the audience swayed to the carol. The curtains closed and the bare house lights were switched on by Miss Hindshaw. There was a complete hypnotised silence for a few seconds, and then the applause was roof-cracking.

The two reporters gave Thomas strong sincere handshakes.

'The Ancoats Miracle Play, eh?' said the one.

'If anybody ever shouts "Give us Barabbas" at Easter, it'll be your lot for sure,' said the other.

The children poured out through the old manor house door, laughing and singing and nudging each other into the gutter. They went into the night; their noises became muffled, then faded.

He stopped for cups of tea, handshakes and Merry Christmasses with his colleagues, then he too cycled into the miserable night. Christmas Eve had barely started, but he knew Christmas was already dead and gone for the children. From what he'd gathered, Christmas Day was for the grown-ups; they visited each other with bottles of beer and played cards for pennies all day; there were usually fights over cheating towards the end of the day.

He only guessed how his colleagues would spend Christmas. Dick and Kitty and their children would spend the time opening presents; they secretly bought each other twopenny knick-knacks from jumble sales throughout the year; then wrapped them and hid them. Miss Cowgill would sit in her latticed windows and read the verses from Christmas cards. Charlie would be calling in on people and having a drink and a mince pie put in his hands; he'd told Thomas that a lot of people expected him to call in on them. Miss Hindshaw would probably read extracts from Tyndale, Ascham, North, Camden, Sidney and Lyly, writers who were writing when Ancoats Manor was being built; it would transform her into a beautiful young maiden in a fresh magnificent log-burning hall bedecked with boughs of holly and mistletoe and smelling of cooked venison killed in the Ancoats greenwoods. The two reporters would be laughing their pints down in a beerhouse, and calling him an idiot.

But the approach to Christmas had been wonderful; there were the achievements of his department store grotto and his children's theatre pageant plays. He remembered the young girls as they became grandmothers and passed the Bo Peep bonnet to each other for their hour in bed; there was Vera from Soft Furnishings, Olive from Haberdashery, Amy from Slumberwear; their eyes had flashed in the winking coloured lights, but he had never had the courage to ask them to go out with him. He remembered the boys and girls in the audience wiping snot and tears from their faces with their sleeves and frock hems.

Finally, there had been Alker. The boy had grabbed his arm after the curtain had closed.

'I start on New Year's Day, sir. Fairey Aviation. There was twenty, and I got the job. 'Twas easy. We had to write a short composition on what country we would like to visit if we was given a ride in an aeroplane, and I wrote ancient Greece and got in all them names you've told me.'

Thomas was cycling to a dead Christmas. He would sit with his mother; there would be no excuses for going out, none at all. She would give him a pair of woollen gloves and a pair of woollen stockings; she always did. He would give her a pair of slippers and a bottle of eau-de-cologne; he always did. But at least there'd be voices from the wireless this Christmas; it might stop his mother from talking about the wonderful Christmasses she and her husband had had before he was born.

She was standing outside the doorway in the cold and the dark when he reached home. She was shivering.

'Oh, Thomas, I'm sick with worry and waiting. What have you been up to? What have you done?'

'What's the matter?'

'A policeman's been. He wants you to go down to head-quarters immediately. Thomas, what have you been up to?'

Thomas didn't know what he'd been up to as he cycled into the city. Perhaps the two clergymen had reported him for blasphemy or sacrilege; after all, he'd put his plays on in a district where they drew blood for religion. And then it dawned on him. It was theft from the railway stables, although his boys had assured him the stuff would be returned before the horse or the railway police missed them.

It was all hustle and bustle in the police station. There were bits of tinsel over the 'Wanted' posters, a sprig of mistletoe over the sergeant's desk, and a Merry Christmas sign on the door marked 'Interviewing Room'.

A burly policeman pulled a scruffy little man towards the door to the street.

'Where you taking Fred?' asked the desk sergeant.

'Across the road to buy him a pint before we slam him in the cells. After all, it's Christmas, sergeant.'

78

'Usual is it, lead off a church roof?'

'Aye, he never changes.'

'Merry Christmas, sergeant,' chirped Fred, as the policeman pushed him out through the door.

Thomas wondered if they'd buy him a pint before they put him in the cells. He gave his name and address.

'Aren't you the lucky one, mate,' said the sergeant. 'We asked a bobby to call and let you know the gold watch was yours. Nobody's claimed it. We thought you'd like it in time for Christmas.'

# Learning was in fault

Was it seven or eight years? Thomas lost count. At the time he had started the children's theatre, he had also started trips to the Manchester Ship Canal. Here he was given permission to take his classes on board the many big ships on the alley-alley-o. On deck they sketched the ships, cranes, shunting engines and storage warehouses. He taught them geography; where cargoes came from, where cargoes went. Sometimes the captains, if they weren't busy, would talk to them about their own countries. They learned about bills of lading, certificates of origin, and empire preference. But always they had to earn their trips to the Ship Canal by learning a poem: 'Quinquereme of Nineveh from distant Ophir', 'To the lonely sea and the sky', 'Sweet and low, wind of the western sea'. A boy was picked at random, and if he didn't know the poem the trip to the Ship Canal was cancelled, and the boy had let his class down, which resulted in a playtime scuffle.

Likewise they had to learn poems to earn a bus ride to Platt Fields. Platt Fields had a lot to offer, and he dipped into his own pocket for the bus fares.

There was a gaunt granite statue of Abraham Lincoln.

Shoot if you must this old grey head,
    But spare your country's flag, she said.

They then had to sketch Abraham Lincoln, after which he told them why the statue was in a Manchester park. When he talked about the American Civil War he was General Grant leading the troops to victory at Chattanooga, or an Ancoats cotton worker starving to death for lack of Southern cotton.

Beyond the statue was a small chapel in which Oliver Cromwell had worshipped:

He who would true valour see, let him come hither;
  One here will constant be, come wind, come weather.

Platt Hall was a gallery of ladies' costumes of the past. In here
on wet days he would read them Alexander Pope's 'Rape of the
Lock' and they would laugh at the amusing bits.

Cutting through Platt Fields was the ancient Danes' Nico
Ditch, their territorial boundary with the Saxons. Here he could
almost frighten the boys with his graphic descriptions of Beowulf's fight with the monster Grendel.

There was always a play in rehearsal or production at the children's theatre, but they had to be bloodthirsty plays. The boys'
favourites were *Julius Caesar* and *Macbeth* on condition that
whereas Shakespeare played his battles off stage, they would play
them on stage. A few girls from the girls' school had joined his
theatre group, and Thomas was forever amazed that they, boys
and girls, could learn difficult lines and long speeches.

With, in addition, his many lessons on Greek democracy and
art, his lads were getting a good education through adventure;
they were also, when the time came for them to leave school, getting good jobs. They wrote 'Ancoats' in flourishing roundhand.

At Pauldens, he was recognised and valued as the display
artist, and he was given the adjoining horse stables for a studio.
They had been last used in the haberdashery days when horses
delivered to Moss Side, Rusholme, Fallowfield and beyond.
They were filled with painted plywood ducks, chickens, piggy-
wigs, baa lambs, squirrels and something-to-crow-about
cockadoodle-doos. There was also, kept hidden in a dark corner,
a naked wax model woman. He talked to her, and sometimes
smoothed his hands over her with his eyes closed.

His life was full and busy. He had no time, he told himself, for
a real woman. But at night in bed he wanted a real woman desperately. He went to sleep always determined to do something
about it the next Saturday. There was Mary from Toys, Eileen
from Kitchenware, and Jessie from the Counting House; they
smiled at him, but he could never find the courage to ask them
out. Rebecca Ginsberg from Artificial Jewellery was different.
He felt sick at his own cowardice when he saw her, and he made a
point of passing the artificial jewellery counter many times.

Rebecca was beautiful and small; she had smooth, slightly oily

81

skin, with tints of winter-sunset summer-daybreak colour in her cheeks; her hair was raven black; her eyes were deep; her teeth were white and showed when she smiled. Sometimes he lay awake all night thinking about her.

Thomas didn't have the courage to look her in the eyes and ask for a date; instead, he wrote a poem asking if she would meet him on Sunday at nine outside the new Central Library in Peter Square; the poem said how beautiful she was. He asked Ida of Electrical Fittings to give it to her. And Enid of Ladies' Wear brought the answer, and it was yes. He couldn't believe it.

She wore a green velvet jacket and skirt; on her head was a green velvet fez with a tassel. In a Medusan sort of way, although for the entirely opposite reason, he was half afraid to look at her.

The city had nothing to offer on Sundays. No theatres, coffee bars or cinemas were allowed to open by law. Churches and museums were open, but they were not the places to take a lively Jewish girl. On impulse he bundled her on a train bound for the Derbyshire hills; they were the only two passengers without thick boots and haversacks. They got off at Castleton and joined a conducted tour down the caverns of the Blue John mine.

The guide's carbide flare lit up the stalactites and stalagmites and seashell fossils in the rocks. The guide told how the Romans had lowered British slaves to work in the mine till they died digging out Blue John crystals for brooches and ornaments. Thomas hoped it would interest Rebecca with her working in Artificial Jewellery and that.

'Poor slaves,' she whispered, and gripped his hand tightly. She held on to his hand, and they now walked hand in hand swinging hands.

The guide went on to say how the battered fossil of a sabre-toothed tiger had been found in the rocks, and Thomas wished the tiger would roar so that he could grip her all the tighter. He would have killed the tiger bare-handed for her, but there was no need for the tiger. Rebecca pulled him back from the group and into the prehistoric darkness.

'Kiss me!' she breathed in his ear.

He kissed her, but it was a quick shy kiss.

'And now hold me round the waist and kiss me properly,' she whispered again. He did, and with all his strength.

'Hey, I didn't say bruise my lips and break my back.'

This was love! The conducted tourists could go away and take their carbide flare with them. They could seal up the mine. He could die with his love for her; die there in the blackest of blackness beneath a mountain. He undid her blouse, and put his hand on her breast, feeling a hard nipple between two of his fingers. Her lips tasted sweet. She pushed him back into the crowd.

'Make sure there isn't a bulge showing in your trousers,' she laughed. But the bulge had gone; it had all happened to Thomas when he felt her breast.

They returned to the city on a train full of maps, haversacks and muddy boots. This time it was her idea to take him on a trip. The bus took them through Cheetham Hill, where the poor Jews lived, to Broughton Park, where the rich Jews lived. And there in this Sunday-night England was a fish and chip shop open for business. It was called 'Lapidus' and the fish and chips were fried in oil, something Thomas had never tasted before. His mother, like everybody else, fried them in fat. If he suggested oil, she'd tell him to go and fry his face in it. Thomas and Rebecca sat on a seat at the bus stop and ate their fish and chips from the *Jewish Chronicle*. Behind them, seven poplar trees were silhouetted by the cloud-glow from the distant city lights.

Sunday after Sunday they returned to the Blue John mine. The guide got to know them and stopped asking the others where those two people were.

Thomas was a pound short of the money he needed to buy Rebecca two Blue John ear-rings. His mother always left money carelessly around, and, dashing out one Sunday, he helped himself to a pound note which was being used as a bookmark; she would never miss it; she left all sorts of things in books, and sometimes didn't even know where she'd left the book itself let alone the bookmark. The ear-rings added to Rebecca's beauty.

She undid her buttons and allowed him to put his hand on her breast, it was firm, and it heaved, and her nipple stood hard between his fingers.

'How fair and pleasant art thou, O love, for delights. This thy stature is like to a palm tree, and thy breasts to clusters of the vine; and thy mouth like the best of wine!' he sighed in her ear.

'And best adjust your palm tree before the carbide lamp shines on us,' she laughed.

'Take me seriously, Rebecca, please.'

'I always do,' she said. 'His left hand is under my head, and his right hand doth embrace me. There now!' She pushed him away.

'I knew it would happen; I hoped it wouldn't happen yet. I wanted it to happen, and now I'm sorry it's happened,' she said. She was crying as they ate their fish and chips.

'Why?'

'Oh, Thomas, don't you know why? It would take more than just loving a Jewish girl and knowing the Song of Solomon to make you a Jew.'

'Then what would it take?'

'About four thousand years for me to tell you, that's what it would take. I love you, Thomas, but I couldn't take you home. And you couldn't take me home. Imagine telling your mother you wanted to become a Jew!'

'I'd probably make a better Jew than a Christian,' he said. A bus drew up and she jumped on it without warning. The bus rolled away.

He never saw her again. He learned the next Saturday that she had quit her job without notice. The staff office refused to give her address. None of her workmates knew where she lived. But Thomas used his brain, or tried to. He looked up all the Gins-bergs in the Kelly's Directory of the Central Library. There were lots of Ginsbergs, and he worked out a Ginsberg route to take them all in. He cycled the route on the nights he was free in the hope of seeing her in one of the streets.

On Sunday evenings he caught a bus and sat on their seat opposite the Lapidus chip shop; after a time he would go in and buy some fish and chips. Eventually Mr Lapidus became friendly with him.

'You're not from here?'

'No. Moss Side.'

After a few more weeks, Mr Lapidus started to greet him, usually in front of a shop full of customers.

'Now here's my customer come all the way from Moss Side for the fish and chips of Joe Lapidus. How's that? Didn't I always tell you my fish and chips was the best for miles?'

'So I write and tell my brother Sammy in New York,' said a customer. 'He's got his own yacht.'

If only Mr Lapidus hadn't made such a show! If only he'd treated Thomas like an ordinary local Jew, then Thomas would have continued going there, and maybe sooner or later he would have met Rebecca again. But then – the thought enraged him – but then she might have been with another man in her green velvet fez with the tassel.

He sighed for the love of a lady; he slept badly at night; he needed a woman to love, and a woman who would love him back. Smoothing his hands over a wax model was no substitute.

It was Easter, and he hated Easter; there was no school, no Ancoats, no anything for a week. It was an unproductive period of time which ended with a death, and that's how he felt. His mother put two hot cross buns in front of him.

'Thomas, I've been waiting for two months, and I'm still waiting.'

'What for?'

'For you to own up that you stole a pound note from *Romance In Naples*.'

'But I didn't.'

'But you did. Now look me in the eyes; never mind looking at the picture of your father; he won't help you; he saw you steal it.'

'I borrowed it. I'm sorry. I meant to pay it back. Here it is.' He offered a pound to her, but she looked away and held a handkerchief to her eyes.

'Keep it. I wouldn't touch it. You stole it from me.' She sniffed into the handkerchief. 'And years ago you used filthy language to me and stole a shilling. Oh, Thomas, what's going to happen to you? I lie in bed all night and weep for you. It's coffee that's changed you, I know it is. You used to drink tea like everybody else, but then you went on to that foreign muck. Tea is natural, but coffee isn't. Coffee makes you think of women, and women make you think of sex, and sex is dirty, and that's why men steal. Coffee can send a man to the gallows, Thomas. Go back to tea.'

He had to get out of the house. He would spend the day in the new library, in the great dome where books echoed clatter-clatter-clatter and the merest cough went cough-cough-cough, and shoes squeaked on the white rubbery floor. But his friends were there waiting for him; Aristotle, Chaucer, Marlowe and Dryden; and they never complained about coffee.

His humour returned to him in time for him to say 'Good

85

morning' to the Owens College gate. On an impulse, he turned into Brunswick Street and stopped outside Professor Eldo Rhado's phrenology shop. His mother's words ran through his mind: 'Oh, Thomas, what's going to happen to you?' What was going to happen to him? Of course phrenology, palmistry, was a lot of phoney wizardry like teacups, the stars in conjunction, salt over the shoulder and walking under a ladder, but he was tempted to see the professor or the princess; they would tell him something; even if it was something to reject or avoid. An undergraduate beat him to it. The young chap was obviously an undergraduate for he had hidden his university scarf in his raincoat, making him look as though he had an oversized bosom. No doubt he wanted to know if he'd pass his examinations.

Thomas read all the postcard advertisements in the window. After quite a long time, the young man came out. He blushed when he saw Thomas. 'I thought they might have Plato's *Republic*,' he said; 'but they haven't.' Thomas went in the shop like going into a dentist's.

Both the professor and the princess were behind a table. They looked alike and must have been brother and sister, both small people with yellowish complexions, except the man's hair receded whereas the woman's hair was long, black and straggly. He coughed nervously, and was about to bring up the subject of phrenology and palmistry, but, damn, another student walked into the shop; this chap had books under his raincoat, and his large bosom was square.

'Yes, sir?' asked the professor.

'I've come about the desk you've got advertised in the window,' said Thomas.

'Very good, sir. Here it is.'

There was a small but sturdy desk behind the table; it was a writing desk, the flap came down to write on, there were three drawers, there was a top ledge for books. Thomas wanted it.

The professor and the princess led him to the desk.

'It belonged to a Doctor of Philosophy over the road,' said the professor. 'He's now gone up the Amazon – '

'Where he'll meet a good woman and marry her and they'll live a happy life together,' chipped in the princess.

'Just feel the wood, sir.' The professor smoothed the tips of his fingers over the writing top. 'It's oak, and oak is a wise wood, a

86

clever wood, the wood of the ancient druids. This, sir, is a hard-working ambitious desk.'

The princess followed one of the grains with her finger. 'It will always be with you, and for a long time to come; it'll last for years.'

'A man behind a desk is a man to be reckoned with,' said the professor. 'It makes him important.'

'People show respect to a man with a desk throughout his long and happy life,' added the princess.

Thomas paid two pounds for the desk, with an extra ten shillings to have it delivered on a handcart. He carried on to the Central Library.

But he was unable to concentrate on any book; his mind was on the desk and on the things the professor and the princess had said. Yes, he had become a man of importance. He liked to walk down the majestic Elizabethan stairway of Ancoats Hall, especially if Miss Hindshaw or one of his classes were at the bottom looking up. He liked to walk down the equally grand Victorian stairway of Pauldens, with its old-fashioned gas lamps hanging side by side with electric lamps, and its shiny mahogany counters, especially if Mr Wingate was waiting at the foot of the stairway to tell him how appropriate his jolly jumping elephants looked in the Trunk and Suitcase Department. He was surprised he had managed without a desk in the house for seven years; he needed a desk; it wasn't a luxury, it was a necessity. He needed a desk to mark homework on, he needed a desk to make white cardboard stage models on, and then paint them; models of Dunsinane Castle and the Senate in Rome; models of his Christmas grottoes, Neptune's caves, Robinson Crusoe's island, the Snow Queen's palace. He slammed his book closed, slam-slam-slam, and went home early to see his desk.

'If you ask me,' said his mother, 'it's only fit for firewood. Falling to pieces, it is.'

'It isn't. It's quite sturdy.'

'Probably crawling with woodworm.'

'That desk, mom, was made by Joseph the carpenter of Nazareth.'

'Thomas, that's blasphemy! And it being just two days off Good Friday!' She disappeared into the scullery.

He sat down at his desk and rubbed the palms of his hands

across the top. Why had he opened his big mouth?

    She returned after about ten minutes with a cup in her hand. 'Here you are, Thomas, I've made you a nice cup of coffee and chicory. And I'll get some nice wax polish in the morning.'

# Circling round

There was trouble in the playground. Charlie Macgregor hadn't arrived, and Dick went out to settle the hash. Thomas waited.

'Trouble?' he asked when Dick returned.

'Ach, I had to send Powner to hospital with a couple of lads as escort, and him with a dislocated shoulder. Sure what'll the little sods think of next?' He poured himself out a whiskey. 'Would ye know, Thomas me fine feller, there were six of them to push Powner into a midden and put the lid on him, and for no other reason than that he was a convert.'

'Religion, religion!' said Thomas. 'Will it ever stop?'

'Sure this wasn't religion. This was because his parents had converted from gas to electricity, and them saying his house was trying to be posher than the other houses. His face was covered in tea-leaves, and a dislocated shoulder! Charlie would have fixed it in a jiffy if he'd been here. But would ye know, me boy, if a kid was drenched with the rain and said it was raining, he'd have his teeth knocked out by some who said the sun was shining. I'll blow the blooming whistle and get 'em into their cells.'

It was a lover and his lass,
　　With a hey, and a ho, and a hey nonino,
That o'er the green cornfield did pass,
　　In the springtime, the only pretty ring time,
When birds do sing, hey ding-a-ding ding:
　　Sweet lovers love the spring.

Over the singing in the hall, Thomas tried to read Longfellow's 'Village Blacksmith' to his class. It was difficult because there was an urge to read it to the rhythm of Miss Cowgill's song.

'Please, sir, what's a blacksmith?' asked Pieroni.

Thomas wasn't sure whether this was a genuine question or the start of classroom crosstalk. A locomotive pooped, shunted, and sent wagons clanking. But another noise jumped up through the window, a different noise. The lads jumped up on their desks to look out. Thomas too was forced to walk down the room and look. Charlie Macgregor had arrived on a motor bike; it was a Panther, a big machine which made a crowding churning noise. Thomas got the kids back on their seats.

'A blacksmith shoes horses, but horses are becoming a thing of the past – '

'Except for winning money on the two-thirty at Castle Irwell, sir.'

'Horses are dying out as a means of transport. Today it is the internal combustion engine, which Mr Macgregor has kindly demonstrated out in the playground. The mechanic has replaced the blacksmith. Now, how the internal combustion engine works is ...' He picked up his chalk and drew a cylinder and piston on the blackboard and went on to explain how the mixture of petrol gas and air forced the piston up the cylinder until a sparking plug caused an explosion and pushed the piston down again. After reading 'The Village Blacksmith', he had intended to start 'Hiawatha'.

There came another noise; a noise which even interfered with the singing in the hall. He was about to explain the purpose of the outlet valve when a barrel organ started to play outside the school. Once again he changed the subject.

'Grab your sketching pads and follow me!' he ordered. They stampeded after him. They formed a circle around the organ grinder, and the man looked terrified. Thomas gave him some money from his pocket and the man pulled his organ away from the school, followed by the class.

The class was told to sketch him, and the man began playing again, looking very pleased and proud. He was perfect for an elderly Italian; a long grey moustache curved upwards and beyond his cheeks; his nose was large and Julius Caesarish; his eyes dark and deep. He wore a trilby hat with a wide brim; his overcoat, which went down to his ankles, was military, no doubt Italian military; his boots were much too big for his feet. His barrel organ had paintings of roses and gondolas. He played the well-known drinking song of Verdi.

Thomas asked the organ grinder to tell his class the name of the man whose music he had been playing. Before he could answer, at least four boys shouted 'Giuseppe Verdi!'

'Hey, hey!' smiled the old man. 'So you gotta little Italian boys, eh? I play again.'

'No, thank you,' said Thomas. 'But perhaps you'd tell them a bit about Verdi?'

'Was a great-a baggy-arsed man Giuseppe Verdi, eh? Was-a born Roncole. Was-a taught-a da musica Milano. And oh da poor district dat-a man come from was-a terrible, eh? Nothing like-a dis.' He swept his arms towards the cobbled streets and squalid houses around him. 'Ancoats fit-a for de Pope compared to-a Roncole. And-a da clothes what he-a wore, well, I would-a be dressed like-a de Prince of da Wales to da rags what he-a wore. And-a da food ...' He put his hand to his mouth as though to eat, then looked and saw it was an empty hand, and he shrugged. 'Food? Der was-a no food. But-a from dis come da most-a beautiful musica. Der was – '

'*Rigoletto!*' shouted Pieroni.

'*Trovatore!*' shouted Granelli.

'*La Traviata!*' shouted Robino.

The old man pointed both his hands to touch the middle of his chest, and made a deep bow to Thomas, with a great happy smile on his face. 'De boys – dey good Italians, *signor*.'

This had been wonderful for Thomas; better than any class-room lesson; the sketchings and the music, but most of all the organ grinder relating talent to poverty and the slums. He gave the old man all the money left in his pocket.

Thomas saw the organ grinder again when he was cycling home down Every Street. The man was leaning against the shafts; he was patting his chest as though in pain. Thomas got off his bicycle and asked him if something was the matter.

'It is-a my heart. It is-a nothing, *signor*. It is-a my heart. It is-a pulling dis-a thing all da day. It is-a turning da handle all da day to make-a da musica. Maybe I live. Maybe I die.'

'I'm pulling it home for you,' insisted Thomas. 'That's the least I can do. Then you've got to see a doctor.'

In spite of the man's pushing him away in protest, Thomas knocked on a door and asked if he could store his bicycle in their lobby; he had to help the old man.

He gripped the two wooden shafts and pulled the organ over the rough cobbles and up the steep brews towards the Italian part of the district. He had to stop for a rest many a time. The old man seemed to recover; he flourished his hat many a time to passers-by, and some actually put pennies in it.

They arrived in Jersey Street, where red hair gave way to black hair, white pimpled faces to smooth brown ones, fat features to thin features. There was one girl leaning in a doorway. She wore a light and loose pink frock; her round breasts were visible through it. Her left arm leaned against the doorway; her right arm was curled at the back of her long tresses. She was beautiful, with the beauty of a consumptive, but she looked sad and tired. Thomas found out later that she'd been stirring ice cream in the tubs since daybreak.

'Hey, Giovanni, you gotta son, eh? You never said you had a son. *Sente*! *Suo figlio, è inglese*. What you pay him for wages? *Come si chiama?*'

'She want-a know your-a name, *signor*.'

'Thomas Davies,' answered Thomas, giving her a very shy smile.

'Angelina Maria Pirelli is mine,' she said. 'Hey, mister, you come and give my tub a stir sometime maybe, eh?' Then she laughed. '*L'asino del organetto!*'

Thomas arrived at the old man's house. '*Tante grazie*! *Molto grazie*!' bowed the man. And Thomas returned to pass Angelina again.

'Ah, *l'asino del organetto*! *Benvenuto*! He make a big fool of you, Tomaso,' she laughed. 'He always getting people to pull his *organetto*. He always say he got a poor ticker. Tick-tock, run up the clock, eh? Don't you believe it. Strong as mine. You want to feel my heart beat? Come here and feel my heart beat. *Vuoi toccare mia mammella? Mia mammella*! *Bella!*' She beckoned him, but he said goodnight and walked as fast as he could, not daring to look around, until he reached the house where he'd left his bike.

'And sure what d'y'mean, left a bike? You didn't leave no bloody bike here, sure that's the truth,' said the grizzly man who answered the door. It was the same man he'd asked if he could leave it. 'Kathleen!' the man shouted down the pram-filled lobby. 'Did a feller come and leave his bicycle here at all? There's a fancy-talking galoot at the door saying 'twas left in our custody.'

'There's only the penny-a-week burial club man ever brings a bike here, and that's on Friday, and he'd hardly likely to be leaving it here now, would he?'

92

Thomas had to walk home, but he didn't notice the walk; he wasn't even distressed at losing his bicycle; he thought of Angelina.

'Now isn't that what becomes of not staying aloof?' said Dick when he told him of events. 'Stay aloof from it all, will ye? As a matter of fact there's a good opportunity for ye to get well out of it all.'

'What's that?'

'The Education Committee have been on to me to try and get ye to transfer to a nice posh school in Burnage, now how's that for a chance to escape? No more stolen bicycles, eh?'

'Why do they want me to transfer?'

'Ar, me fine feller, and would ye not be knowing? 'Tis our job record. There's more of our little sods getting jobs – and that when the blooming country's in a depression – than any other school in the city. Now up in Burnage, they own their own houses, they're ratepayers, they're taxpayers, they keep the Education Committee going. Now isn't it right that the boys from Burnage should be getting the jobs in preference to the kids from Shit Creek?'

'I'd like to take an hour off to get my bike back, Dick.'

Thomas went straight to Honest Amy's in Great Ancoats Street. His bicycle was leaning against three other bicycles.

'And what can I do for you, chuck?' asked Honest Amy.

'3179863,' said Thomas, patting the saddle.

He was glad to be back on his bicycle; man and machine knew each other, knew each other's faults and foibles. Thomas decided to turn the half hour into an hour, and on an instinct cycled to the art gallery in Mosley Street and chained his bike to the railings.

It was Angelina, and there she was. He knew he'd seen her somewhere before. Only she was the little priestess of Aphrodite in Lord Leighton's painting *The Last Watch of Hero*. He stared at the painting. 'Hey, mister, you come and give my tub a stir sometime maybe, eh?' The picture gave him confidence, and he needed confidence; he had no luck with girls, and he wanted a girl; he wanted Angelina.

It was easy for his bike to choose a route back to school which went up Jersey Street. She was there. She was puffing at a cigarette in the doorway.

'Hey, hey! Here he come again, the *organetto* donkey! *Allora, l'asino del organetto*! He come looking for Angelina, yes? *Benvenuto*, Tomaso!'

She'd remembered his name; that gave him the courage he needed. He managed to stutter out an invitation to meet him on Sunday.

'Sure, sure! Why it take you fifteen minute to ask me? I got a tub to stir.'

It had been agreed for her to meet him outside Pauldens at noon. Noon was the earliest either of them could make it, for he'd been asked to turn in and dress a holiday travel window, and she said she dare not miss mass at Saint Michael's. He fastened the last port-hole to the plywood steamer, and rushed out to wait for her. He stood outside his window and listened to the drill commands being shouted from the Territorial Army depot across the street; he tried to pick out Sergeant-Major Macgregor's voice.

She strutted towards him, and she was lovely, and he was thrilled; she was dazzling. She wore a red and green silk head-scarf on her long black hair; her blouse was blue, and she filled it well; her round hips easily carried a black and yellow striped skirt, which went no lower than her knees; her silk stockings shone; she wore long glass ear-rings; there was a perfume around her.

'Well, I am here. You did not think I would come, eh? *Non pensi che sono una bella ragazza italiana, vero*? Have you ever been out with a beautiful Italian girl like me before? No, *non penso così*! So where you take me?' She pointed to one of the travel posters in his window which showed the Eiffel Tower. 'Where Tomaso take Angelina, eh?'

'I'd thought of the Blue John mine,' said Thomas. The black blind darkness under Mam Tor mountain was the only place in which a man could kiss a girl in the daytime on Sunday, and it need not stop at lips to lips.

'Mine? What is that? Do you want me to dig for coal?' She put her hands on her hips.

'I thought you'd be interested. It has connections with the Romans. They made brooches for their sweethearts,' he stammered. His confidence was ebbing fast. But before anything further could be said by either of them, there was a loud roar from a motor bike, and Sergeant-Major Macgregor swung out of the barracks gate on his Panther. He stopped and smiled, and chatted about nothing in particular.

'Ah well, laddie, I'll noo be breaking up a romance between you and this lovely wee lassie, so I'll be awa noo.' Charlie prepared to kick his pedal starter.

'Where you go?' asked Angelina.

'Awa hame, bonnie wee thing.'

'To your wife?'

'Ach no! I bide on my own.'

'I have never been on a motor bicycle,' she said. 'It must be one big fright, eh? Fast, eh?'

'Hop on, lassie! I'll give ye a wee spin round the houses and back.'

Angelina sat astride the pillion and put her arms around Charlie. He kicked the starter and the bike roared. '*A riverderci*!' she shouted above the noise, and away they roared down the road.

Thomas spent the rest of the day at his desk, which had been polished like glass by his mother, constructing a model set for *King Richard III*. There was murder, battle and bloodshed in *King Richard III*.


Thomas felt no enmity towards Charlie for stealing his madonna. A touch of sarcasm was his only acknowledgement.

'Young Lochinvar,' he sneered at Charlie. 'His steed was the best.'

'Aye, laddie! Get yourself a Panther, for you'll never pick up a cannie lassie on the crossbar of your bicycle.'

    O cuckoo! Shall I call thee bird,
      Or but a wandering voice?

Miss Cowgill had set her own tune to the poem, and it sounded good from the hall; but it smarted Thomas's pride. He was a wandering voice, just a wandering voice, and nothing but a wandering voice. Girls ran away from him. He would never bother with girls again in his life. He was miserable, and Pauldens was the first to suffer.

Mr Wingate took him to the meat counter, put his arm around Thomas's shoulders and pointed up to a large cut-out pig.

'That there pig seems to be sneering, lad. Not smiling contentedly, if you know what I mean.'

'Perhaps it knows it's going to be put in a sausage machine.'

'Aye, lad, happen it does. But let's crack on it likes the idea. Get your paint brush out, lad, and give it a smile, a big broad smile.'

Rehearsals for *King Richard* suited his mood; it was full of frustration, anger and bitterness. Thomas never ceased to be amazed how well his groups could learn their lines; he had to prompt a lot, but they got through the most ambitious plays, and the young audiences understood and enjoyed them. The *Manchester Evening News* and the *Manchester Evening Chronicle* photographed and praised them. Raglan Street got in the newspapers, and Charlie Macgregor was able to apply for football boots. He got them, and his teams began to win a few games, draw a few games, lose a few games.

Perhaps sensing his unhappiness, Miss Cowgill invited him to her Saturday night after he'd finished at the store. But it wasn't outside the Cosy Corry; it was outside the Mersey Hotel. She was as cheerful as ever as she took him by the arm and led him inside.

'Of course the Cosy Corry long since switched to talkies,' she said. 'And if I'm going to keep my little cottage, well ...' she shrugged. 'I'm what they call a pub pianist. But I make them happy, they enjoy listening to me, they sing along with me, and I get a couple of pounds for doing it; so isn't that what life's all about, Mr Davies?'

This night she didn't sing to them; she sang to him, as she had once done in the Cosy Corry. Every love song was directed to him; and he blushed so perfectly that women in the lounge would shout 'Hey, look at him!'

'Give us another, Fatty!' the men shouted.

'Every time she bumps, she bounces!' was another popular yell. Miss Cowgill smiled and played and sang, played and sang.

Quite frequently somebody offered to buy her a drink, but she refused because she didn't drink; however, she pointed to Thomas, and at one time there were six full pints of beer on the small round table before him. He was relieved when she sang general songs like 'The Lullaby of Broadway', but even then she managed to blow him a quick kiss at the 'goodnight, baby' point. He didn't remember saying goodnight to her. All he remembered was pushing his bike home, and wobbling, and falling over his bike, and being sick in the road. He woke up in the morning in his bed; he'd slept in his clothes. His mother was downstairs slamming cupboard doors, and the church bells were ringing so merrily.

Once the scholars left school, they never returned to tell Thomas how they were getting on; he usually found out from Sergeant-Major Macgregor.

Charlie always gave school leavers a talking-to about joining the Terriers. He said it would make real men of them. He promised he would look after them; that they'd get smart uniforms; that they'd be allowed to handle and shoot rifles like they'd seen in the cinema; that they'd get a shilling for a Sunday morning parade; that there were annual camps at places all over Britain; they'd see the world free of charge; ach, even get paid for it into the bargain. And every girl agreed that there was something about a soldier which was fine, fine, fine. Many of the lads joined up as Sunday soldiers; and it was therefore from Sergeant-Major Macgregor that Thomas learned that his boys, now called 'youths', had started work at Imperial Chemicals, Kelloggs Corn Flakes, the Royal Infirmary, the Manchester Ship Canal, Fairey Aviation, the Midland Hotel, the London, Midland and Scottish Railway, and the town hall. All this news was good, for there was great unemployment in the land.

An opportunity came for Thomas to see some of his old scholars one Sunday morning. He'd been asked to turn in and dress a gardening window. It was an eye-catching splash of green and yellow with red dots here and there. Glad-to-be-back dickie-birds flew from piano wire; there was a huge chuckling sunflower; there was a gang of naughty weeds running away in terror. There were masses of green raffia for grass. Thomas was about to push a lawnmower into its artistic place; then he heard a military band playing 'Blaze Away' somewhere down the street.

He knew the parade would have to pass his window to get to the barrack gate; he knew Sergeant-Major Macgregor wouldn't be able to resist an 'eyes right'; he knew he would be giggled at. He dropped down as flat as he could behind the lawnmower and covered himself with a raffia mat. The bugles and drums got louder as the parade approached. He gave the lawnmower a push forward to make doubly certain he was well hidden by it. His chin banged down on a metal bar, and he realised his tie had become entangled in the mower blades.

The parade passed the window. Through the blades he could see marching boots and khaki trouser bottoms. He had been taken prisoner by the lawnmower. It was an awkward situation; he could move the mower neither backwards nor forwards; his tie had jammed it. He felt around for something to help him, and his hand gripped a pair of hedge-pruning shears; these might do. Slowly and slowly he manoeuvred the shears until he was able to snip through his tie at the knot. He jumped up so glad to be free that he knocked over six smiling bunny rabbits, which knocked over the chuckling sunflower, which hit against the flock of homecoming bluebirds. Everything in the window fell, except the retreating weeds.


'Please, sir,' said Murphy, 'what d'y'think of Herr Hitler?'

The question came as a surprise to Thomas. He had been standing by the bust of Homer in the Athens Room, and had been telling them how the Greeks had fought with the Trojans for ten years, and all because the beautiful Helen had left her husband to go off with her fancy man Paris, although Thomas told them he guessed it was only an excuse for war; perhaps because Troy was taxing every Greek ship that passed through the Dardanelles. He'd given them his own graphic description of the fight between Hector and Achilles, using verbal expressions nearer to the Boathouse Stadium than to Homer. Eventually he had got round to Alexander the Great.

'The Greek states were at loggerheads, hating each other's guts in fact, and Greece, with all its new ideas of democracy, philosophy, science and art, looked like crumbling and being lost for ever. But Alexander came on the scene and forced them into a unity, but it was the unity of a vassal country, and to some extent the glory that was Greece was preserved. Unfortunately, Alexander did it with ruthless massacre, indescribable bloodshed and

98

fear. Now I want you to ask yourselves – ' It was at this point Murphy interrupted.

'Please, sir, what d'y'think of Herr Hitler?'

Thomas knew very little about Herr Hitler, he'd heard the name of course, but his mind was too filled with the sacrifice of Prometheus, the humour of Aristophanes, the upside-down observations of Herodotus, the gallivantings of medieval pageant plays, the swift murders and sweet words of Elizabethan dramatists, the putting on of plays, the painting of happy ducks and ambitious piggy-wigs to be bothered about what was going on in the world. He never had time to read the newspapers, and his mother always switched off the news on the wireless because she said the news was always nasty.

'Tell me what you know of Herr Hitler?' he asked.

'He's the king of Germany, sir. He makes all the Germans wash themselves, and he gives them money so's they can go in beerhouses and sing beerhouse songs.'

'He's a bloody dirty rotten stinking shit-house!' shouted Nally.

Some of the boys jumped to their feet and threatened each other with their fists. Thomas noticed quite a lot of them were bandaged up; no doubt it was the result of another street fight; nothing out of the ordinary. But they started to move towards each other. There could not be a fight in the Athens Room; they would break everything to smithereens.

'Stop!' he yelled. 'What's it all about?'

'We smashed up the bloody blackshirts last night outside the Gaumont picturehouse,' said Nally. 'There was bloody Oswald Mosley farting from his mouth about the British Union of Fascists. And there was thousands hitting and belting each other, and the police came on horses, and there was a lot taken to hospital, and there was blood all over the road. It was a good fight, and it lasted a long time, sir.'

'Marvellous, isn't it?' said Thomas. 'Marvellous! They don't allow Sunday cinemas or theatres for entertainment, but they can be used to incite bloodshed.'

'Yeh, but it was a good thing, sir,' said Nally. 'We knocked the shits out of the blackshirts.'

'Did you buggery!' shouted Murphy. 'And you're a bloody traitor; you sided with them yids from Cheetham Hill. And it's

99

not Oswald Mosley, it's Sir – bloody "Sir" – Oswald Mosley. And his family owned this museum, and he should be lord of the bleeding manor, he should.'

'Shut your trap!' shouted some of the boys.

'I'll not shut me trap. Mr Davies asked a question about Herr Hitler and I'm answering him. We're starving in bloody Ancoats, but they're not starving in Germany because Herr Hitler is getting rid of the yids what starved 'em. And I'll tell ye summat about yids; they feel up Christian girls' skirts but won't marry 'em.'

'Why do they call him "Herr"? Is it because he's got hair on his chest?'

'He only thinks he has. And he thinks he's God.'

'That's daft. Only God thinks he's God.'

'There's no God!' shouted Nally.

'Hey, shut up, Nally. God'll get you if he hears you saying that.'

'There's no God!' repeated Nally. 'There's only people, and it's up to us to tie our own bloody bootlaces. There should be no rich while others is poor. And there should be no such things as Germans and Russians. And there should be free Vimto. And there should be free love.'

'What's free love?'

'Not having to give a tart a penny so's you can put your hand up her clothes.'

'That's what yids do.'

'Then let's all become bloody yids.'

'Me dad says England's got to go one way or another.'

Although sickened at some of the ideas, Thomas was not altogether displeased that threats of stupid violence had been reduced to stupid argument.

'Please, sir, who do you stick up for? Herr Hitler or Comrade Stalin?'

'I don't stick up for either. I'm a believer in democracy.' He spread his arms. 'And this is where it all began.'

'In this room, sir?'

'No, Alberto, in ancient Athens.'

'I thought you said they had slaves, sir.'

'I doubt whether they'd have accepted you even as a slave, Alberto. Anybody who can mistake this room for the city of

Athens would hardly know if he was pouring out wine or water.'

'But they couldn't have been democratic, sir.'

'I said democracy began there; it's still got a long way to go; we're still striving for it. And when I saw you lot preparing to half kill each other five minutes ago ... we've got a lot of striving ahead of us.'

'But Herr Hitler's only going to do what Alexander the Great did, sir. He's going to save Europe by uniting it.'

'And so's Comrade Stalin,' said Nally.

'You ask me what I think of Mr Hitler and Mr Stalin; I don't know. It may be that they will enrich the world with art and music and beauty and happiness, which includes food to eat and nice homes to live in. Time will tell. But one thing I would insist upon is that these two gentlemen be made to account to their nations and present themselves for re-election with a choice of other candidates every four or five years. Let the people judge them by what they do, not what they say. Oh, and let me give you all a few words of advice. When you're old enough to vote, exercise your democratic right to vote; weigh up all the arguments and vote; because if you don't vote you can't complain even if the government puts you in chains. It's better to put a cross on a piece of paper with a pencil than a cross on each other's cheeks with a razorblade. And if you must fight – and it seems you little beggers must fight – don't fight for another man's ambition; better to fight for Helen of Troy – '

'Or Betty of Tutbury Street.'

'Or Una of Dunn Street.'

'Or Clara of Angel Meadow.'

'Hey, Collins, what d'y'know of Clara?'

'That she might be all right for the meadow, but she's no bleeding angel.'

'I'll smash your bloody teeth in when we get outside. She's spoken for, she is – and by me.'

His lesson on ancient Greece over, Thomas raced up the street to the dinner hall. Miss Hindshaw handed him a cup of tea.

'I was listening through the door,' she said. 'I thought for one moment the gods were going to end up in a heap of dust. I thought poor old Homer was a gonner for certain.'

'He just closed his eyes and hoped for the best,' said Thomas.

101

'He was in a thousand pieces once,' she went on. 'Just look at all the joins.' Homer's bust was a network of joins. Miss Hindshaw smiled at first, and then a look of anger came into her face.

'Years ago a small boy of nine pushed it over. The police arrested the boy, and the magistrate ordered him to be given eleven lashes.' She'd appealed for the boy; she'd told the magistrate that it was an accident and the bust could be repaired, but the magistrate had insisted the sentence should be carried out with severity because he would not tolerate vandalism. 'So the poor little boy was lashed, and fainted, and was revived, and the lashing was completed. But the worst was when his mother called to thank me. She said my kind words had decided the magistrate to order the lashing instead of imposing a fine for damage which would have had to come out of her purse. I spent months sticking Homer back together again.'

The night had been wonderful beyond Thomas's wildest dreams. Six hundred children had gone home into the dark thrilled, frightened and enchanted by *Richard III*; and why not? The play had more than its share of ghosts and battles, and battle scenes had been acted on stage. There had been a slight shemozzle when the curtain was lowered between Shaughnessy, playing Richard, and Robino, playing Richmond, because Shaughnessy claimed Robino had deliberately hurt him with his wooden sword when he was killing him. But everybody had gone home; even Miss Hindshaw had asked Thomas to lock the Hall up; and proud Thomas wandered around the rooms and down the great stairway feeling very much the lord of the manor, hoping that in the quietness he might see the ghost of some beautiful maiden, the daughter of some long dead baron. Nothing happened. He locked the door and walked out into the night. The locomotives were shunting and clanking across the road. He put his cycle clips on.

Two men rushed out of the dark and dragged him and his bike away from the steps.

'We're going to make a bloody example of you, Moses,' said the one man. 'They're going to find you beaten up to buggery tomorrow morning, and it'll scare the shits out of 'em.'

'Bleeding bolshie, aren't you, Comrade?' said the other.

'He's worse than that. He's a bleeding yid. Aren't you, Moses?'

102

One man had a cut-throat razor in his hand; the other had a bicycle chain over his shoulder ready to bring down. Thomas's instinct was to grovel and beg them leave him alone. 'Please let me go,' a silent voice urged in his chest.

'Name's Davies, isn't it?'

'Yes,' he squeaked, and the silent voice told him to beg for mercy.

'That's it then; Davies is a yid's name; the bloody town's full of 'em. Answer me when I ask you summat! Bloody yid, aren't you?'

There was a red flash in Thomas's brain. He was about to shout 'yes'.

'Jewboy, bleeding four by two, right?'

Again he felt compelled to shout 'yes'. But before he could open his mouth, the chain lashed down over his shoulder. He felt he'd been cut in two. The chain came down once more; this time across the small of his back. He felt sick; his groins and knees lost feeling. There was a sharp streak of a razor on his cheek.

And then he lashed and kicked back. He swung his arms and fists in all directions, and kicked and kicked. He shouted all the bad language he'd ever heard his boys use. He wasn't aware that he was hitting a person, just that he was hitting, and that whatever he was hitting would have to stop moving before he stopped hitting.

The razor man backed away and settled for bringing his boot down on the spokes of the bike. Thomas wrenched the chain from the chain man, and swung it and swung it at the man. The chain man crumpled up on the steps of the Hall; he didn't move. The razor man ran away.

Thomas dabbed his cut cheek, and limped away with his wobbling bicycle. He was weak and frightened.

His mother couldn't speak when she saw him. She helped him into bed and bathed his injuries.

'It was my fault, mom. I ran into the back of a coal lorry. My eyes must have been dazzled with all the lights on the stage; I didn't see it in the dark. I'll be all right.'

He spent the weekend mending his bike, and fortunately it was the Whit week holiday; he had only two duties to fulfil that week, and those were to attend the Scholars' Walks.

On Whit Monday, all the Protestant churches marched through the city to Albert Square; on Whit Friday the Catholics did the same. His boys would be in both processions, and he felt it important to let them see he supported or was at least interested in them.

The Protestants were usually led by a sailor band; the Catholics by the bagpipes and kilts of McSweeney's Pipers. Both processions filled Albert Square before the town hall; the Monday crowd being blessed by the Bishop of Manchester; the Friday crowd by the Bishop of Salford. And there on the steps of the town hall, beneath the statue of Agricola, both bishops gave their blessing. The Protestants sang 'Abide With Me', the Catholics sang 'Faith of Our Fathers'.


Thomas whistled the seduction song from Mozart's *Don Giovanni* as he cycled home. There had been a music concert at the Hall. Miss Hindshaw had persuaded some musicians to give up their time to play the popular classics, and Miss Cowgill had volunteered to sing a few songs. He had rigged up a microphone and speakers in the other rooms because so many people had turned up that the theatre was overcrowded. Occasionally he stopped whistling in order to sing the song. He didn't know the language, but he found that by singing the names of all the Italian boys in the school, it seemed to rhyme and scan. His mother was waiting at the door.

'My goodness, Thomas, where have you been and what have you been up to? I never know when you're coming home. I sometimes think you've forgotten you've got a home. There's a visitor to see you, and he's been waiting for ages. You should stay at home at night; you never know who might call.' Nobody ever called, but Thomas let it go.

The young man in the parlour jumped smartly to attention and held out his hand. 'Hello, sir! I've a train to catch at midnight, but I couldn't go back without seeing you. I hope you didn't mind me finding out where you lived.' The youth hesitated. 'Course I bet you don't know who I am, sir?'

'Yes, you're Hetherard Saar, the boy who didn't know Goethe was a German.'

'That's a relief. I thought you wouldn't remember me.'

'The Archbishop of Canterbury.'

'1118 to 1170.'

104

'I asked him if he'd like a nice duck egg, with him having to travel by train,' chipped in the mother.

'Fine, thanks; honest!' Saar turned back to Thomas. 'I've come to say ta for helping me take an opportunity when it came my way, sir. Like you was always saying to do. I've been in England on a few days' leave, straightening things up and that.'

'Come to England? Leave?' asked Thomas.

'Aye. I'm a real German now; we live in Germany. They wrote and offered me dad a good job. He was a chemist at Holt Town muckyard, sorting out metals and calcium from the middens. Wears a white coat now, and does the same sort of job in a laboratory. Germany paid our fare back and gave us a house in Hamburg. Then I charged for the guns like you said, and sat my examination for the Luftwaffe, and passed.'

'Luftwaffe?'

'German Air Force, sir. We started on gliders. We've got internal combustion engines now. They said my handwriting was perfect, and my general knowledge, particularly about England, was first-class. And thanks to Mr Macgregor, I took to drill like a duck to water. I've just passed out as an officer and a pilot.'

Thomas shook his hand with enthusiasm. 'Congratulations! I'm as pleased as if I'd done it myself.'

'Well, you did, sir.' The young man looked up admiringly at the picture of Thomas's father. He stood on tiptoe and smoothed the wings on his dad's tunic. 'Those were the days, eh?' he said.

'I've told him about your dad,' said Thomas's mother.

Saar handed a large wrapped-up parcel to Thomas. It looked as though it might be a tray or a picture. It was in fact a picture.

'I thought you'd like this, sir.'

It was a framed photograph of himself in a very smart uniform being handed his flying insignia by a stout smiling high-ranking officer.

'That's General Goering congratulating me and giving me my pilot's wings.'

'Thank you. I shall treasure it.'

'General Goering once flew with Von Richthofen.'

'Did he, by gosh! D'y'hear that, mom?'

His mother took the picture and held it against the wall near the picture of her husband.

'It'll go nicely just there,' she said. 'Perhaps you can nail it up in the morning, Thomas.' Then turning to Saar: 'Are you sure you wouldn't like a nice duck egg? And we have coffee. I suppose you drink a lot of coffee. A nice cup of coffee?'

Hetherard Saar had to leave for the station. Thomas looked at his watch to make sure of the time. He'd walk to the station and see him off.

'You always said aviation was the thing to get in, didn't you?' asked Saar from the carriage window. 'The first job you helped one of us get was at Avro.'

'What sort of aeroplanes will you be flying?'

'They're called Heinkels, sir. They're used for transport.'

Thomas looked at his watch again. Saar burst out laughing.

'I'm bloody glad you've still got your watch, sir.'

'So am I. But what's funny?'

'We gave it you for Christmas; the class did.'

'You didn't. I found it if you must know.'

'Only because we left it where you'd find it.'

'On the cobbles?'

'We were peeping. You wouldn't believe it, sir, but it took you three nights before you noticed it. We had to keep picking it up after you'd gone. Once we thought you were going to cycle over it and smash it. You missed it by a cat's whisker.'

'You couldn't possibly have bought this. It's real gold.'

'Oh, we knew that. But, y'see, one of us found it on one of your educational trips to the Ship Canal, it was with a lot of other watches down below on one of the ships we went on. We guessed it was meant to be smuggled ashore and therefore nobody on board would dare report it.'

The railway guard blew his whistle and waved his green flag. The train hissed, blew off steam, grated its wheels on the tracks, and pulled out of the station.

'*Auf Wiedersehen*!' shouted Saar.


He's up each morning bright and early
    To wake up all the neighbourhood,
To bring to every boy and girlie

106

His happy serenade on wood.
To serenade your lady, you find a tree that's shady,
    And listen to that tick-a-tick-tick tick-a-tick-tick,
Happy little woodpecker's song.

# Dismal tidings

Metro Vick's canteen was filled to the brim. The thousands of women and men on the night shift had sung their heads off to 'Washing on the Siegfried Line' and 'Run Rabbit Run'. Paddy Reilly, who was now a leprechaun air raid warden who carried binoculars with which he watched young women getting undressed in their bedrooms when he should have been searching the skies for enemy bombers, had been the best turn of the workers' concert.

'And would ye know,' he told them, 'haven't I, Paddy Reilly meself, invented something that'll totally revolutionise air raid precautions? Would ye be wanting to know what it is? Ah well, I'll have to keep me voice down for even walls have ears – sure they haven't got eyes and noses but they've got ears – and we'd not be wanting enemy agents to be finding out, would we now? Well, 'tis a jet black electric light bulb, so that when ye switch on the whole blooming room is plunged into thick black blackness.'

After that he caused a thousand moist eyes with 'Danny Boy'. There was a roar of applause like trains starting from stations. He bowed low, jumped off the stage and grabbed Thomas's arm.

'Come on now, Mick; sure I know of a pub down in a cellar that keeps open after hours.'

Thomas was relieved his mother had gone to bed when he finally got home. He'd had one over the eight and was a bit tiddly, and he'd something to tell her, but not in the middle of the night; not when the beer was talking.

But the next morning was different. Everything was an overture for what he had to tell her. Outside in the street little girls were skipping and singing a skipping rope song:

They say that the Luftwaffe's leaving Berlin,
   Bound for old England's shores,
Laden with land mines and bloody big bombs
   To blow in our windows and doors.

'The war has completely destroyed Sunday,' said his mother. 'What with Sunday cinemas and children playing in the street and comedy programmes on the wireless, it's blasphemy.' She placed a plate of porridge before him. 'Mind you, I knew the war would come. From the very day they knocked the head off Jesus in Whitworth Park, I knew we'd be punished. And it's never been put back on.' She looked up at the picture of her husband. 'And I don't know what on earth your dad would say if he knew I couldn't get brown sugar for your porridge.'

Thomas pulled a brown envelope from his inside pocket. The letter inside had already been seen by Dick Wilson; it had been seen by Mr Wingate; he'd even shown it to his naked model. His last job at Pauldens had been to put the wax model on war work by dressing her in a siren suit with a tin hat on her head and a gas mask slung over her shoulder to advertise fashionable gas mask cases at reasonable prices.

'I've got to report to Lord's Cricket Ground, London, on Wednesday, mom. Here's my warrant.'

'Oh, are you playing cricket? I didn't think – '

'It's a kitting-up centre. I'm in the Royal Air Force. I passed the tests three months ago. I'm accepted for air crew.'

She sat down; she looked amazed, staggered. 'But you never told me. Why didn't you tell me?'

'I'm telling you now. There was no point my telling you before and having you worry.'

'The Air Force?'

'Yes.'

'Flying?'

'Yes.'

She pointed to the ceiling. 'Up there?'

'Best place to do it.'

'There's no need to be sarky; you're too sarky; there's no call for it.' She looked up at her husband's picture. 'I shall be on my own.'

'It can't be helped.'

'Does the Air Force know I'll be on my own?'

'I had to fill in a next of kin. I suppose they do.'

'You can't go, Thomas. I shall write to the Air Force and tell them to think again.'

'I don't think they'll take much notice.'

She looked shrewdly at her son, and then smiled a knowing smile as though she had got him and his Royal Air Force cornered.

'Ah, but tell me this, Thomas, with all your fine education, who's going to darn your stockings or wash your vests, shirts and underpants? Go on, tell me.'

'I'm quite sure they've got guidelines about things like that.' Thomas put his arm around her. 'Look, mom, teaching isn't a reserved occupation. Charlie Macgregor was called up the day after war was declared. They'd have called me up sooner or later, be sure of that. Better to follow dad's tradition, eh?'

'And go getting yourself killed? He was very selfish when he did that. I'll stick my head in the gas oven if anything happens to you.'

He gave her a squeeze. 'It won't. I promise.'

Thomas wasn't too sure about not getting killed. The night before he'd signed up, he'd seen Errol Flynn in *The Dawn Patrol* and it had made him feel brave; but coming out of the old school in Dover Street the next morning, he'd not felt so courageous. Dover Street School had been honest; it had given up its claims as an educational building, and was now solely devoted to putting every man and woman in Manchester who was eligible for war service on its register. The conscripted school was just across the road from his university, and in the next street to the phrenology shop. Feeling cold and shivery after signing his name, he was tempted to visit Princess Eldo Rhado, not that he believed in palmistry; but there was a queue of three outside the shop, and he cycled away.

For the first time in his life, Thomas saw the sea, the real sea. He'd painted it enough times in holiday windows; wavy lines with playful fish jumping in circles; and he'd created a Neptune Christmas grotto, using the same Neptune a month or two later to advertise swimwear. And now he was sent to the real sea. His Initial Training Wing was at the Grand Hotel in Torquay. Here he was taught navigation, meteorology, astronomy, morse code and military law. He was a pupil back in a shining classroom with a view of the sea from the windows, and holding up his hand and saying 'sir'. His school cap had a white starched flash above his cap badge, and his school motto was 'Per Ardua Ad Astra'. He sometimes pretended his Ancoats scholars were at this school. He enjoyed every minute of it.

There was better to come. From Devon he was sent to Marshall's Flying School. Here in another classroom he was taught theory of flight and the internal combustion engine; but it wasn't all classroom; in between blackboard lessons he flew in a yellow Tiger Moth from Newmarket racetrack.

His instructor was an old-school-tie type of English gentleman who treated and talked to his Tiger Moth as though it were a thoroughbred horse; he patted it, and Thomas wondered if he occasionally gave it lump sugar.

'Come on me beauty, let's show this cadet how well you can jump clouds,' he would say to the yellow flying machine, and to Thomas he would say: 'Always use the throttle; never the whip.'

His instructor sometimes took the country squire bit a little too far, but Thomas didn't mind; the man was a good teacher. Several times they landed in a flat Suffolk field where there were no anti-invasion stumps. The instructor would jump out of the cockpit, leaving Thomas to keep the engine ticking over, and level his gun up to shoot rabbits. He claimed that his machine had accounted for more rabbits than any other Tiger Moth in the King's service.

'But you've got to be sharpish, or the Home Guard might shoot you first.'

Flying was easy, and flying was fun. Thomas looped the loop. He climb-climb-climbed until the engine shuddered and stalled, and it was on its back; then he dived, switched on his engine again, and pulled back the joystick. For split seconds he hung suspended over Christ's College, Cambridge at three thousand feet, and it amused him to think that he'd done something John Milton had been unable to do when he was a student down below. In the evenings, he wandered between the clean brown and grey steeples, turrets and towers of the colleges, or took a boat out on the river and read poetry as he drifted; always Cambridge poets, and often Milton:

Look homeward Angel now, and melt with ruth.
And, O ye dolphins, waft the hapless youth.

111

But Thomas never looked homeward. He did not go home; he didn't want to go home. He had a conscience about not seeing his mother, but after this new life of freedom he couldn't bring himself to get a warrant for the Manchester train. His mother would expect him to sit by the fire and listen to her. It would be duck eggs and porridge. He could use those warrants to see England for the first time. He could visit the actual places he'd only read and taught about from books – Bath, Canterbury, Durham, Whitby, Stonehenge, Oxford. In Oxford he saw the colleges which his matriculation had qualified him to attend, but his mother's sobs of loneliness had forced him to turn down. He could sit and listen to music in the great cathedrals. In London he visited St Paul's, Westminster Abbey, the British Museum – the British Museum and the real Elgin Marbles, the real art of Phidias. He stood on Westminster Bridge and checked the time on his gold watch with the chimes of Big Ben. Manchester and Moss Side, not today, thank you! He was far from hapless; hapless was the last thing he was; he was the luckiest man alive!

He received his wings with the brass band and bagpipe ceremony of Cranwell College, and he assumed his luck would now change; he was trained for active service.

'Active service?' said his commanding officer. 'What the hell are you mumbling about, Davies? You're too old for that kind of nonsense. The Wellington bomber is not equipped with a rocking chair. No, Davies, you're being shipped off to Canada as a navigation instructor with the Empire Air Training Scheme. You're a teacher, and you're going to do all your fighting with a blackboard and a piece of chalk.'


The *Queen Mary* was a gorgeous lady. She sneaked out of the Clyde to begin her unescorted voyage to New York. A letter had reached Thomas just before embarkation, and he leaned over the deck rail to read it. It was from Dick Wilson.

'I'm so grieved to tell you Miss Cowgill is dead. She apparently committed suicide. Her room had been sealed and the gas taps were full on. It looks as though she had been playing the piano until she collapsed. There was sheet music of Chopin on the stand, and there was a photograph of a soldier from the last war in front of her. She was playing to him I suppose. I may be wrong, but it was something I'd always guessed from little things she sometimes said. I think she was going to be married, but he was killed on the western front. She blocked it all out with her non-stop singing and piano playing. Perhaps this new war brought it all back to her. She left no note except the sheet music. It was that popular version which is all the rage, and she had underlined "on broken wings my heart has taken flight". In her young days she had been a prize pupil at the Royal College of Music. Kitty says she is a war casualty right enough.

'It must have seemed strange to you, as indeed it did to me, how a funny little fat woman could get some of the toughest snottiest young hooligans in Great Britain to sing those cissie songs of hers. Kitty thinks she has the answer, and Kitty may be right at that. She says that Miss Cowgill was everybody's mother, if that makes sense to you. She was the perfect mother the kids all wished they had, and Kitty may not be far wrong. Just think of the Ancoats mothers. They are drab and aged long before their time what with starvation, disease, deaths in the family, and worry over survival. They are always shouting, swearing and fighting with their husbands and the other women in their street. In many cases they didn't even want their kids, but their religion threatened them with hell fire if they prevented them. They were dull and broken in spirit. Maybe some of our scholars knew inside themselves that they were only born as a result of rape or an alleyway poke. Miss Cowgill was their jolly daytime mother.

'I have a lot of new schoolmasters now. They have been brought out of retirement; the sound of the yelling of kids has come, and the slap of the strap can be heard in our land. As I write to you, the new singing master has got them singing "Hearts of Oak". I would give anything to hear a cuckoo song.

'I had hoped to have Raglan Street to myself. I had visions of getting the bottle out and my feet up on the desk in an empty school because the town hall began a complete evacuation of children to the wide open countryside far from the night bombers, but within a fortnight the kids, lice and all, had returned to their stinking hovels. Most of them complained that the fresh air of the Pennines made them ill; some said they were chased by mad bulls; and one kid complained that he had no sooner stepped off the train on to the platform than a bird flew over him

113

and shit on his head. He wouldn't leave the station until the next train home.

'Kitty sends her love, and Paddy Reilly says "slainté".'

Thomas was angry with the letter. Dick should not have written to him. He didn't want letters; not those kind of letters. He crumpled the pages up and dropped them down into the sea. 'Damn, damn, damn!!' Within minutes he was asked to attend on the ship's master-at-arms, who gave him a strong reprimand. Those written pages he had been seen to drop overboard could be telling the enemy that the *Queen Mary* was on course for New York. But the reprimand was cut short by another breach of secrecy.

The hundreds of cadets on the decks below, who were on their way for training, began blowing up their stocks of military issue contraceptives, tying them tightly with string, and letting them blow away like balloons in the wake of the ship. A trail of these contraceptives drifted in a line on the ocean wind. A stern voice on the tannoy ordered it to stop. The trail of French letters, said the voice, could easily be spotted from the periscope of an enemy submarine or the binoculars of a Fokker Wulfe Kondor, and the unescorted vessel had to rely upon speed and non-detection. Besides, added the voice, it was undignified for the greatest ship in the world, bearing a royal name, to be the launching platform for such objects.

The big ship sailed east by south-east on a zigzag course.

# Terms and tides

The French Canadian village of Ancienne Lorette was eight miles outside Quebec City; it was in dull countryside, and its only history was that the Indians had surrendered it to the French without a fight, and the French had surrendered it to the English without a fight. The airfield had been an Iroquois settlement in the days of Champlain, and Indians were employed to keep the school and barracks clean.

The school was a collection of light airy classrooms with sliding blackboards; the desks were a bright yellowish brown, new and shiny. Somewhere in the complex was a large dance hall, a bowling alley and a bar. Ice cream and Coca Cola were everywhere. It was not a bit like Raglan Street, but then this was a school for war.

Thomas liked to go for a quiet evening drink in a small white-washed tavern. The woodwork was scrubbed clean; there was a sign forbidding bad language or hand-gripping; there were pots of salt on the tables to sprinkle into the beer; the customers were lumberjacks and wore lumberjack shirts and bobbed caps. Some of them wiped their eyes with their sleeves when they sang 'Quand Il Neige Sur Mon Pays'.

His colleague was Aussie, who in fact was a New Zealander; they called him Aussie to annoy him, and Aussie always took the bait. 'I'm not an Aussie, I'm a New Zealander, and I'm in the Royal New Zealand Air Force.'

This would invariably bring a reply, particularly from an Australian, of 'What d'y'mean "in"? You are the New Zealand Air Force; you're all they've got.'

Aussie was slightly younger than Thomas; his navy blue uniform made him stand out; but a cultural bond grew up between the two instructors when they discovered the North American shirt. Unlike British and New Zealand shirts, which had to be put on over the head, with only four buttons on the top half, and stud holes for loose collars, the Canadian shirt had the collar attached and buttoned all the way down like a jacket. They also discovered a toilet liquid called after-shave lotion which was meant to be slapped on the face after shaving. Notices in all toilets ordered airmen not to leave after-shave lotion lying around; the Indians would drink it. Another novelty which Thomas and Aussie marvelled at was called a juke box; drop a nickel in the slot, an arm would bring out a record, and Bing Crosby would sing.

On Sunday mornings Thomas preferred to be on his own. He caught an electric train and walked up through the pinewoods to the top of Montmerency Falls, and here he would sit and puff away at his pipe. And his daydreams became real. Before him were Alker, Cathcart, Shaughnessy, Robino, Frascatti, Haynes, Saar, Pieroni, Kelly, Murphy and all the others. What price the Manchester Ship Canal now; here was the Saint Lawrence River. And the statue of Abraham Lincoln in Platt Fields; why, some miles south over the river was the soil Lincoln had walked on! It was here, all here, the history of a beginning; not the history of an ending like Ancoats. Yes by golly, he'd even teach the little sods French!

'What do you do up at Montmerency Falls every Sunday?' Aussie asked him.

'Oh, I, er, take a class of scholars.'

Flying Officer Davies's first class at Ancienne Lorette was on astronomical navigation. The cadets at the desks before him were only about four years older than the Raglan Street school leavers. He felt shy at first and tossed a piece of chalk up and down in his hand. Then the bust of Homer came into his mind, and his confidence returned.

'This morning I'm going to talk about heavenly bodies,' he began.

'You mean like Betty Grable?' said a voice from the back. There it was, the old familiar start to a lesson.

'I would suggest that the young gentleman who said that might care to make himself known to me after class. A few hours marching on the parade ground with full pack before daylight might help take his mind off Betty Grable and direct it towards the twinkling stars who will be keeping him company at that time of the morning. Yes, gentlemen, it's the twinkle-twinkle variety I'm going to talk to you about. In a few weeks' time you may not know what they are, but you will certainly know where they are. You will know the names of the stars in the sky, and you will learn that the sub-stellar points of these stars will give you a fix, and a fix will tell you where you are on one of those nights over Europe when your compass and radio have been put out of action by forces beyond your control.'

He began to dot shapes on the blackboard.

'Now this constellation is Orion. You will see the head, shoulders, belt, sword and legs. He was a mighty hunter in ancient Greek legend. He was also a big drinker, and on one occasion forced a young lady named Merope to go to bed with him – '

There were cries of 'shame' from the class.

'That's what Artemis thought. She was goddess of the hunt, and she fell in love with Orion. But one goddess wasn't enough for Orion – '

More cries of 'shame', and 'the bastard deserved to die'.

'He fancied her seven friends, the Pleiades. And he chased them all over the place. So Zeus, his commanding officer, changed the girls into doves. Maybe Orion had a Spitfire for he still gave pursuit. Zeus then changed the doves into stars.

'Now by accident – or so she said – Artemis let fly an arrow which killed Orion – '

'Aw, what a pity!' said the class.

'She begged Zeus to make her ex-lover immortal, and Zeus changed Orion into a constellation which you see on the board. Well, of course, no hunter is complete without his dog, so here is Sirius by his feet, the brightest star in the sky, much brighter than Rin Tin Tin, for the benefit of the movie-goer at the back. You never get stories as good as this from Hollywood, do you?'

'No, sir,' answered the voice from the back.

It was the custom of Thomas and Aussie to see their graduates off at the railroad depot; excited young men with their brand new brevets, sergeants' stripes or officers' armbands pouring on to the train, laughing, joking, pressing their noses against the carriage windows; noise, noise, noise; going home with pride. To Thomas, it was like his boys scrambling on to the tram or bus for a trip to Platt Fields; there was no difference.

Afterwards, when the train had wow-wowed into the curtain of snow, the two instructors pulled up their greatcoat collars and strolled along the lighted pathways of the Plains of Abraham, usually going no further than the joint memorial to Wolfe and Montcalm. They returned for a few drinks in the Château Frontenac before they too caught a train. There was always leave for them after a passing-out parade, and their leave was always spent in New York.

They sat on the tall bar stools, and Thomas brought a letter from his pocket to read to Aussie. Normally he didn't open mail from home; he didn't want to read news from Ancoats or Moss Side; often he carried an unopened letter in his pocket for six months before throwing it into the Saint Lawrence. This time, however, curiosity had got the better of him and he'd opened it; it was from his mother:

'Manchester was heavily bombed just before Christmas, and hundreds of people were killed. A bomb fell at the far end of the street and knocked several houses down. The blast cracked two panes of glass in your bedroom window, but I have had them fixed. It cost five shillings. Prices are terrible. I was so angry at the time that I nearly took the photograph of that young boy shaking hands with Mr Goering down from the wall. Then I remembered he had been one of your favourite scholars. I hope he wasn't one of the Germans who cracked the window. Five shillings is a lot of money, and I think the Germans ought to be made pay for any windows they break.'

The two men doubled up with laughter.

'Write and tell her we've just sent a hundred men off to go and break German windows,' said Aussie. The remark seemed to turn the men serious.

'They say school-days are the best days of your life,' went on Aussie, 'and I suppose the lot we've just seen off have enjoyed themselves here with the beer and skittles and juke boxes. But what happens when the train stops?'

'They get on a ship,' said Thomas.

'And when the ship reaches port?'

'They get on another aeroplane.'

'Probably for the last time.'

'Aye,' said Thomas, and took a long drink.

'They fly forgotten.'

'What's that?'

'From the hymn,' said Aussie. 'Time like an everlasting

stream bears all its sons away; they fly forgotten as a dream dies at the opening day.'

Thomas looked at his gold watch: 'I think it's time we – '

'You're not really keen on going back to England, are you?' asked Aussie. 'This royal throne of kings, this sceptred isle, this precious stone?'

'I don't need an Aussie – '

'A New Zealander.'

'A New Zealander to tell me that. You don't know my England. Dirt, soot, cobbles, blood, snot, juvenile fornication in cat-shit filled entries – and a mother who suffocates me. Precious stone!'

Aussie had touched a sore spot. He had lost interest in England and the war. There had been one occasion when he'd felt like demanding his return; it was when he'd heard that Avro of Manchester had built a new bomber which was to be called the Manchester. He felt it was his duty to fly one. But there had been so many crashes in tests that they'd changed the name to Lancaster. His enthusiasm had broken in the wreckage of the Manchester. He told Aussie about it.

'What's in a name?' asked Aussie. 'For that matter, did you know that everybody at Ancienne Lorette calls the Anson the "Davies" bomber?'

'Because it carries no guns, drops no bombs, and is yellow?' snarled Thomas.

'You're right, Thomas,' said Aussie, grabbing Thomas's wrist and looking at the gold watch. 'It's about time we caught our train.'


Their base in New York was the headquarters of the USO at 99 Park Avenue. Here they got free tickets and passes to everything in the city. They were given New York. They met people they'd only heard of – Tommy Dorsey, Jimmy Dorsey, Jack Teagarden, Cab Calloway, Lena Horne. They became regulars at Radio City Music Hall. They went to every show on Broadway. They went to ball games and on river trips on paddle steamers up the Hudson River. They went up the Empire State Building. They met Captain Glenn Miller after he had made his last broadcast before leaving for England. He was pleased to receive his first ever salute from two British officers.

'And I guess I'll be getting plenty more of them,' he said. 'We're going over there to entertain American and British troops. Hell, half the young men of America must be in England for the fighting.'

Thomas and Aussie made friends with the posh people of Scarsdale, who all claimed their ancestors had crossed on the *Mayflower*. Thomas told them he'd come on the *Queen Mary* which was more comfortable. He walked out with an attractive girl from Wellesley Girls' School, but it was only walking out; he was afraid to kiss her in case she jumped on a bus and took America with her.

'Why didn't you ever kiss me?' she asked when the train was taking her back to college. 'I always wanted you to kiss me.' But it was too late; the train pulled away.

Thomas and Aussie were given tickets for the twenty-eighth anniversary celebrations of the People's Chorus of New York at the Waldorf Astoria. It was packed; it was a big occasion; it was full of music. Thomas forgot everything; he felt important again; then the choir sang a song:

Cuckoo, Cuckoo, we'll dance till the light of day;
  Cuckoo, Cuckoo, we'll dance all our cares away.

Thomas almost fought to get out of the ballroom. He had to wipe tears from his eyes, and was annoyed with himself because there were tears, and he didn't know why there were tears. Aussie followed him.

'New York should mind its own business!' he half shouted. It should not have sung a cuckoo song. It had no right. 'I don't think there are any bloody cuckoos in America anyway.'

'Oh, I'm sure there are,' said Aussie. 'And if there aren't, they can always buy some.'

Thomas said nothing on his way up back to Canada. He heard the ding-ding-ding of level crossings and the wow-wow of the locomotive; he saw the reflection of himself in the window, blurred by fast-moving conifers.

The first night back at Ancienne Lorette settled things for him. He was in an Anson somewhere up the Saguenay. There was no moon, but the stars were shining. And then Satan

120

switched on the northern lights, and everything became frightening and magical. The sky was a rolling mixture of rainbow colours. Everything inside the aircraft changed colour from second to second. The compass needle swung around like a gyroscope. Radio frequencies drifted; what should have been Quebec base in morse code drifted into a dog biscuit programme from Schenectady. They were lost and flying wild. The two engines chanted 'Fly forgotten, fly forgotten, fly forgotten!' The trainee navigator lit a cigarette, which was all he could do. The pilot, a local bush pilot, made the sign of the cross and began to recite out loud:

> Go an' marry some nice French girl
>   An' leev on wan beeg farm.
> De win' can blow lak hurricane,
>   An' spose she blow some more,
> You can't get drownt on Lac St Pierre
>   So long you stay on shore.

Flying in a dream; all Canada had been flying in a dream; he had lost connection with reality; he had forgotten and was flying forgotten. New York had stabbed his conscience with a cuckoo song.

Quebec radio asked all motorists to stop their cars and point them in the direction of Quebec and the airfield with headlights full on. The pilot was able to follow the tiny glistening needles down below. They landed. Wolves were howling around the airfield.

He applied for a transfer back to England. He demanded the right to go on active service.

Aussie also asked for a transfer.

'Europe next stop, eh, Thomas?' said Aussie, and he pretended to give a big yawn. 'How boring; the thought of all those leaves in London and Paris. Still, I won't be on my own; you'll be with me, Pom old boy.'

Thomas's posting came through. It was Education Officer with a promotion to Squadron Leader at the radio school in Calgary. Calgary, way out west beyond the prairies, and at the foothills of the Rockies! He had demanded to get in the war; he was being sent two thousand miles further away from it, and with all the time in the world to get there, for his warrant had been left undated...

'So that you can see a bit of Canada before you go home,' his commanding officer said.

# Lands he could measure

Thomas wandered on his own through the streets of Toronto. There was a shabby old buffalo munching grass in a compound in the park; a museum piece; just one unhappy buffalo. He felt as lonely and miserable as the buffalo.

There was a restaurant called The English Grill in Dundas Street. Well, he'd perhaps meet an English waitress in there. But The English Grill was far from being English. It was a Chinese restaurant, and the waiters were Chinese. And the diners, they were all men, were seated each on his own at small round tables. They were all scruffy and unshaven; it was hard to tell if any of them were English. There was no smell of food, and none of the men were eating food. He asked for a whisky, but he couldn't be served with one for the liquor laws of Ontario were not those of Quebec. He ordered a pot of tea; all the men had pots of tea in front of them; he guessed the Chinese made better tea than coffee. The juke box was loud:

Drinking beer in a cabaret and was I having fun
Until one night she got me right, and now I'm on the run.
Lay that pistol down, babe; lay that pistol down;
Pistol packing mamma, lay that pistol down.

He watched the men at their separate tables. From time to time one would call for a fresh glass of water, or to have his teapot refilled, and the waiters would run to do whatever was ordered. And then Thomas noticed that a man would sneak a bottle from his pocket, and, holding an empty glass under the table, top it up with what he imagined was gin.

The record on the juke box had not finished when a large man staggered into the grill. He had a gun in his hand. The waiters rushed here and there in panic. He shot one of the waiters and red blood splashed on the wall; the waiter was dead. He shot the plate glass window of the grill into shattering smithereens. He turned round and emptied the rest of his bullets into the juke box. The men at the tables scurried under their tables. A Chinaman grabbed Thomas:

'You in soldier uniform. No good. Bad if you caught. You come with me. Quick, before police!' The Chinaman bustled Thomas out through a back-door and into an alleyway. 'Now, mister – run, run, quick!'

Thomas walked quickly. He jumped on a streetcar, and somehow got to the railroad station, where he took any train which was about to move. He finished up in Niagara. He stayed for a few days, spending most of the daylight watching the mighty waterfalls, getting drenched to the skin with the spray, and watching young Canadian soldiers and young American soldiers with their arms around their new wives and not minding the spray at all; indeed looking dreamy-eyed at the half-dozen rainbows.

His warrant was in his pocket, and the absence of a date made him, he felt, an authorised deserter. On impulse he would have travelled right down the United States as far as Mexico, but he only had enough dollars in his pocket to last him a few weeks, and there would be a cap full of dollars waiting for him in Calgary; so he rejoined the westbound train, getting off at Winnipeg to stretch his legs before chugging on to Medicine Hat, Moose Jaw and Swift Current and other places with covered wagon names.

There seemed nothing to Winnipeg except tall buildings on a flat land, but where the city ended was the Red River, and a walk along the banks of the Red River would give him good exercise and fresh air ready for the cigarette-smoke train. The river was in flood and it was a reddish brown. Green shoots of grass were spreading after the melted snow, and the trees were all ready to pop their buds. It was a warm day.

On a seat by herself sat a young woman. A red squirrel ran up and down a maple tree taking crumbs from her. She was a small beautiful girl; the one corner of her mouth rose higher than the other when she smiled at the squirrel. She wore a purple flower-patterned frock and what he guessed was a short beaverskin jacket. He was about to say something to her but she put her finger to her lips for shush because the squirrel was about to approach her for another crumb. And then she smiled at him; she smiled as though she knew him and had been waiting for him. To hell with the squirrel.

'Nice day,' he said.

'Sure,' she said.

'Friendly squirrel,' he observed.

'Hungry one,' she said. 'Just come out of hibernation and I guess he wants his breakfast.'

Thomas was as compelled to kiss her as the compass needle is forced to turn to magnetic north. It was not going to be another Scarsdale. He put his arm around her and kissed her; it was natural; there could have been no other course of action; it was the compass needle. He kissed her long and hard, and she put her arms around him, and her lips replied to his lips.

'I could shout rape,' she said.

He backed away. Timidity returned. 'Please don't. I'll go away. I've a train to catch.'

'I won't shout. Do you think I would?'

'I don't know.'

'I guess you do.'

'Why are you here?' he asked.

'I don't know. Why are you here?'

'It's the direction my feet decided to take; no other reason. Do you often come here? To feed the squirrels and that?'

'No. It's the direction my feet took. Must be over a year. Tell you what; kiss me again; then go off and catch your train. What d'y'think?'

Without a second's hesitation he kissed her again, long and hard. Her kiss was strong and pulling, and her breath was sweet. It all became too public and too daylight; the daylight dazzled. They stood up and walked arm in arm to the main road. She had an apartment in Fort Garry Mansions.

'I'll make you coffee before you go,' she said. 'Take your tunic off. Make yourself at home.'

As he unbuttoned his tunic he looked out through the window. Below him was an old ruined wall, all that was left of Fort Garry.

'What's taken your eye?' her voice said behind him.

'The ruins.'

'Well, turn around. I don't think you'll find me a ruin.'

He looked around. She stood naked, completely naked. He had never seen a naked girl before in his life, and he shivered with excitement. Every curve was smooth and beautiful and inviting to his hands. She was there; she was naked. He took his clothes off and felt no embarrassment; it was the right, the only thing to do. She waited and smiled. He embraced her. This was the first time his body had touched another body; the sensation was like an electric current, a pleasant warm gentle electric current; no, a hot strong electric current! Throughout the night they made love.

His fingers shook the next morning as he tried to put maple syrup on his pancakes; the coffee swirled and swayed in the cup.

'I've got to go to work,' she said.

'Oh, Florence, don't! Please don't! Stay here!'

'I can't. I'm a hairdresser; I've got appointments. I need the dollars. Ever heard of dollars, Tom? But you stay here. Or go for a walk. No, don't go for a walk. Don't ever walk along the banks of the Red River, d'y'hear? Pass time away. I'll be home in the afternoon; my last appointment is at three.'

'Florence, I love you!'

'Say, isn't it crazy! I love you,' she replied, and it thrilled and flattered him. He loved her, and the girl he loved said unmistakably that she loved him, and love is not loving but being loved. She put her arms around him:

'Oh, well, I guess Mrs Macdonald can wait a wee while. She can read a couple of magazines; it'll improve her mind no end.'

Later, Florence decided that Mrs Macdonald could make another appointment or go elsewhere, and it was now Mrs Samuels' turn to read the magazines.

'How long can you stay?'

'Long as I want, I think,' said Thomas, 'except that, like you, I need the dollar bills, and they'll be accumulating for me in Calgary.'

'Hey, I've a good mind to hide your uniform so you can't escape while I'm away.'

'Don't worry; the threat of a firing squad wouldn't shift me.'

She left, and he felt lonely; lonely and stunned. Even though it was her apartment, he was afraid she might never come back. He stared at the ruins of Fort Garry, and watched the sun's shadow changing angles.

But she came back. They made love, and she fried a couple of Lake Superior trout afterwards. Over the meal, she looked seriously at him.

'Tom, you're not a young man; I'm not a young woman. Heck,

126

we're neither of us kindergarten, are we? Yet I'm your first woman.'

'How d'y'know?'

'It was a dead give-away at the beginning. It would be more difficult now.'

'I hope you'll be my last woman, Florence.'

'Oh, yes please; so do I,' she sighed.

'Why the sigh?'

'Tom, I'm married. I'm a married woman. My husband is serving with the Canadian Army somewhere in England. Does that make you feel bad?'

It did. He couldn't answer.

'Because we've committed adultery?' she continued.

'No,' said Thomas. 'All we've committed is love. We've made love because we are in love. More than any other people have been in love; more than any couples at Niagara.'

She laughed. 'I guess everybody says that. But you look down in the dumps, Tom. Why, tell me why?'

'Because your husband is where I should be, in the war. And he should be where I am, with you in Canada.'

'Don't worry; we never hit it off from the day we were married. It was something we should have broken off long before it ever happened. We were both relieved when he was sent overseas; we've agreed on a divorce just as soon as he returns. Now, Tom, how's your conscience?'

'I suppose my conscience is too busy enjoying the trout.' There was silence while he chewed. 'Florence, when it's happened, the divorce, will you marry me?'

'Try and stop me. I want to marry you. Isn't it crazy but I've wanted to marry you all my life, and I never knew it. Well, I didn't know you'd come along, did I? Am I crazy?'

'We both are. That's probably a good basis for marriage.'

'Tom, do you think I'm a whore?'

'How could I?'

'Sure?'

'I just know. God knows how we came to meet, a chance in a hundred million; but we've met, and that's that!'

'I've never done anything like this before.'

'And you'd better not again,' he said, pretending to strangle her.

She grabbed his hands and held them down by their sides.

'You said you can only stay till your money runs out,' she said. 'But you won't need money when you're with me. What do you want money for? See, I'm not a whore!'

'I'll hit you if you use that word again. You're my wife.'

'Suppose you could get a job for a month?'

'Ha, a stay of execution!'

'I've got you a job. Mrs Samuels' husband is something to do with the Hudson's Bay department store downtown. They want a relief man in their display department, holiday relief for a month. You told me last night you'd done that kind of work, so I mentioned it to her. You've got to go down and see them, okay?'

'Okay. Except I can't very well go down or start work in the King's uniform, can I now?'

'No problem.' She rushed into the bedroom, opened some doors and drawers, and returned with an armful of men's clothes. 'Don't worry; he's never worn them. He was sent abroad before he had a chance. And, besides, I paid for them. And they're exactly your size.'

A couple of hours later, Thomas was on the payroll of the Hudson's Bay Company, and was being given his assignment.

The entire top floor of the store was a huge permanent exhibition of the north-western frontiers of Canada in days gone by. There were genuine covered wagons and chuck wagons with pots and pans. There were life-sized models of the men and women who took the sunset trails; the women in shawls and poke-bonnets, the men in beaverskin caps and buckskin jackets. There were Indians in full feather; there were stuffed wolves and stuffed bears. The panoramic background was of the plains and the foothills. There were squaws and maidens making belts of wampum, and hanging out pelts to dry. Two young braves were making a birch bark canoe. Strewn around were muskets, powder horns, concertinas, rolls of calico, blankets and salt kegs, presumably items which the Hudson's Bay Company had once sold or bartered from their log cabin stores. Seated on a wax horse was a wax Mountie.

'Now, this here is the wild and woolly west, pal,' explained Mo Conkergood, his new boss. 'Being a Limey you won't know about such places, but what you see is what it was. Now, we got books with pictures for you to look at, and what I want from you, pal, is a complete renovation job. You might kinda paint a herd of buffalo on the background, for I guess the whole shibang is short of buffalo. And I guess an eagle in the sky; yeh, sure, an eagle. And them wigwams need a repaint job. Guess they was last painted by Sitting Bull with Crazy Horse holding the tin of paint for him. There's a coupla stuffed beavers on the way, once they've been caught. Sure as hell you can't get beavers these days. Make it real, pal, eh?' Mo paused for breath. 'Say, you ain't a conchie, pal?'

'No,' said Thomas.

'Only with you being a Limey in civvies.' He patted his left breast. 'Maybe like me, eh? Trouble with the ticker?'

'Yes,' said Thomas, and he felt he was telling the truth.

Thomas enjoyed the work. In order not to appear incongruous in the exhibition, he bought a lumberjack shirt and a stetson hat. Instead of smoking his pipe at coffee time, he sat on the canoe and rolled a cigarette; he supped his coffee from a blue enamel workingman's can. Mo nicknamed him the Manitoba Kid, and once or twice a child would grab its mother's arm and say 'Look, mam, that one moves.'

Life was as gay as Alouette, the pretty little skylark. He felt more Canadian than the Canadians, and sang cowboy songs as he worked.

He made love to his wonderful wife. He studied library books while she prepared the meals; it was important, he told her, to know all about wavelengths, frequencies and supersonic heterodyne if he was going to become the Education Officer at a radio school.

'All I know about radio is that it has a knob for switching on.'

'And so do you,' said Florence. 'Put your book down and let me switch you on.'

He bought her a wedding ring with his first week's pay to replace the one she already wore. At weekends they caught the train to Lake Winnipegosis and sometimes swam; sometimes rode on the carousels; sometimes ate hot dogs. They were inseparable. Thomas learned all he could about Fort Garry settlement, and Mo asked him to do conducted tours, which put a few more dollars in his pocket.

But there came a night on the pillow when he had to say: 'Florence, darling, I've got to report to Calgary, or they'll be shooting me as a deserter.'

'I won't let them.'

'There comes a time when extended leave becomes absence without leave, and absence without leave can grow into plain straightforward desertion.' He squared an imaginary poster with his hands. 'Five dollars reward, dead or alive, the Manitoba Kid.'

'Five bucks is too cheap. I'd pay ten bucks for you any day.'

'For that price I'm yours. Wrap me up.'

'How do we get there? One of your covered wagons? Or do we take the train?'

'We?'

'Sure, honey, you don't think I'm going to let you out of my sight, do you? With all those beautiful girls of the prairies, and springtime in the Rockies? I'm coming with you. I'm a professional hairdresser. I can get a job and an apartment in Calgary soon as we step off the train. I'll start packing.'

# The love he bore

Calgary High School was on the Heights above the town. It was new, and the roads around it were still unmade. Thomas guessed it had been used as a school about a year before being put in Canadian Air Force uniform and made to stand to attention. The corridors were lined with glass showcases of native animals. It was a fine school, a sunny school, a neat and tidy school; the sort of school his Raglan Street kids should have gone to. The windows on the west side revealed the real but unreal Rockies. The air was the purest he'd ever breathed. It was quiet – quiet apart from spasmodic rifle shots. He followed an arrow which said 'Headmaster', knocked on the door and walked in.

There were two men, an officer and a sergeant, standing at a wide-open French window. Outside was a smooth green lawn.

'Quick, there's another little goddam son-of-a-bitch!' shouted the officer. The sergeant passed the rifle he'd just loaded. It jerked up to the officer's shoulder, and 'bang!' 'Got the tight-arsed little bastard!'

Thomas coughed. The officer still kept his back to him.

'I guess you're Squadron Leader Davies, new Education Officer?'

'Yes, sir.'

'And you shoulda used the Canadian railroad system 'stead o' coming dog sleigh round the Yukon. Still, you're here. I'm Larry Revitt, boss of this coconut stall. This is Sergeant Shabaga. He keeps my rifle loaded. What you are seeing here is the extermination of gophers. I am dedicated to ridding all Canada of gophers. I chalked up six today, but they keep coming. They ruin the trim lawns of God-fearing folk. Up they pop – pop, pop, pop, and nibble, nibble, nibble – then bang goes me gun. It's the only way, buddy. Any time you feel like grabbing a rifle, it's okay by me.'

'You don't really need an Education Officer, do you, sir?'

'Ah no! Y'see, buddy, our kind of radio operators are out of

131

fashion like the archers of Agincourt. This school has turned out some of the finest radio operators in the world. And if dear old Limeyland – you are a Limey?'

'Yes, sir.'

'I thought so. I could tell by the knock on the door. That's a Limey knock if ever there was one I said to myself. Well, if dear old Limeyland had gone under, you'd have needed us with long-range bombers. But it looks like the Canucks are wiping their feet in Europe, and the kind of aeroplanes they need over there are those things made of cardboard called Mosquitoes, which beat as they sweep as they clean. We're out of business, buddy.' He put the rifle to his shoulder and fired. 'Missed the pox-ridden polecat by a mile! You know, Shabaga, we should use hand grenades.'

'Sure, sir,' said the sergeant, 'but that'd be doing more damage to the lawns than the gophers.'

'Good thinking, sergeant. Keep it up and I shall be giving you a brass crown to put over them stripes of yours. Well, my dear old Limey buddy, what happens is that the guys bash out a bit of morse in the morning, then they're free to go to hell after lunch. You'll probably find most of them fishing for trout in the Bow River.'

'I'm no good with a rifle, sir. So what do I do, go fishing?'

'You can do what the hell you feel like doing. If you want to start classes, go ahead. We've even got some sort of an aeroplane you can fly around in if you want to give them air to ground prac-tice. But keep it away from the mountains; it's got no head for heights.'

'Yellow?'

'Goddam right it's yellow; it's a trainer. Why?'

'I've logged a few thousand hours in yellow aircraft. I doubt if I could fly a blue one or a green one,' said Thomas.

'Come to think of it, it might be a good idea if you got a time-table going again. Those airmen are fishing the river dry of trout. Now, gophers is one thing; trout is another. There's Crow and Blackfoot in Alberta; they're big fish eaters. You could prevent an Indian uprising. I'll introduce you to your instructors tomorrow.'

'One other thing, sir.'

'Fire away.'

132

'Can I have a sleeping-out pass?'

'Broad?'

'Yes.'

'Jeez, and I thought you Limeys was a bit behind the door when it came to picking up skirt. Okay, so long as you give her a kiss for me, eh?'

Larry Revitt turned round, and Thomas snapped to attention and saluted. Beneath his commanding officer's wings was the DFC and bar. The coconut man had done more than his share for England.

'Bandits!' shouted Sergeant Shabaga. Revitt grabbed the rifle, turned and fired. 'Goddamn! Missed again! I'll bet the little bugger is burrowing himself clear to the Montana border.'

An hour or two later, Thomas and Florence lay in bed, happy, fulfilled, and in love to a point of impotent weakness. He reached over to his tunic and brought out a letter to read to her. It was from Miss Hindshaw; he had long since explained who the lady was.

'The manor house is deserted since you left. The children's theatre is set out with beds as an emergency casualty centre, but I doubt if it will ever be used, thank God. There has, however, been one important casualty, and I must tell you about it. One lonely little aircraft flew over the town one night. You could hear the engines throbbing the way German engines do. It was probably on its way to Liverpool, or else it was lost. Well, the anti-aircraft people had a new mobile gun, and it went from street to street banging up at the sky. The blast broke all the windows in every street the gun went to, and people came out of their houses and flung pennies at the gun crew and told them to go and play in the next street. Of course there were no real casualties – except the bust of Homer. He was just a heap of dust. There is no way I could put him back together again. Poor old Homer went the way of Humpty Dumpty. Hurry and come back, Mr Davies. We need you.'

'Not as much as I need you,' said Florence, putting her arms around him. 'Do you ever want to go back, Tom?'

'There's no such place as England,' said Thomas. 'And Ancoats, like Troy, is pure mythology.'

He met his instructors the next morning. He had expected lethargy; instead he found enthusiasm.

133

'Mornings are morse,' he began. 'Get them up to twenty-four words a minute. For plain language, transmit them Virgil's *Aeneid* in Latin, then they can't guess what's coming. I'll let you have my book. If they ask for a translation, read them Mark Twain. Send them verses from *Les Fleurs du Mal*; it's sensual enough for them to want to translate for themselves, and, being Canadians, it's as well for them to know French. Teach them not only how to make emergency repairs in the air, but how a radio set works. And if any of you know anything at all about television, tell them about it. It'll help them get jobs when the war's over. We have a band. Can they play more of the Chattanooga Choo-choos and less of the Blaze Aways?'

Larry Revitt was delighted when a week later the band played 'Pop Goes the Weasel' outside his window. Thomas wore his lumberjack shirt and stetson when off duty.


The school was given the day off for the opening of the Calgary Stampede.

'It's chuck wagon racing and bronco busting,' said Florence. 'I know you look the part, but are we going?'

'I've seen and done it all in Winnipeg, remember? I dusted the horse down and gave it a new tail. I gave every Indian a new coat of paint.'

'Then let's go to Lake Louise. It's the most beautiful sight in the world, and we'll have it all to ourselves. What d'y'say?'

They caught the bus to Banff, and there was a sign saying 'To The Lake'; the pathway through the arches of sweet-smelling trees was more enchanting than any Christmas grotto.

Florence had to excuse herself; all the coffee that morning made it necessary for her to pay a call, and the only place was behind the bushes.

'But go ahead down the path. But stop somewhere and wait for me; we've got to see the lake and the glacier together.'

He strolled through the green quietness; the soft, soft, bouncy quietness of the pine needles beneath his feet made it like walking on air, warm cushioned air. Eventually he sat down on a tree stump to wait for her. There was a rustle through the bushes. It couldn't be Florence; her footsteps were too gentle; it must be a ranger; damn!

A giant brown bear lumbered towards him; it was taller and wider than any man could be; it snorted through its shiny nostrils. Its two small brown eyes looked straight at him. Thomas was petrified. He was afraid to blink, twitch or even breathe. He was too afraid to shake with fright. The bear ambled towards him. It brought its paw out and touched his pockets very gently. It sniffed him; he could feel its hot breath in his ears. It searched on the ground near his feet. It grunted. Then it lumbered back into the bushes. Thomas couldn't keep his teeth together.

'Gee, what's the matter, Tom? Can't you talk? Are you ill?' asked Florence when she skipped down the path to him.

'It's a bbb-bbbbb-blob . . .'

She gripped his arm with concern. 'Tom, tell me, what's the matter?'

'I've seen a bear. A great big brown bear. It came. It touched me. Florence, it was a bear!'

'The place is full of bears, I believe. Sure glad it wasn't me though. They beg from people. They're protected.'

'I wasn't.'

'There! That's better! The blood's come back to your face.'

'It isn't like the Hudson's Bay store, is it?'

'No. It's better; it's real; it's fantastic! Come on!' She gripped his arm and rushed him down to the lake.

Neither could speak when they reached the water's edge. It was so magnificent, so silent, so sweeping that they felt guilty just looking at so much beauty; their eyes were inadequate. The lake was deep blue and still. Beyond, and filling the sky, was the great white glacier. The reflection was cleaner than the real. The air was unlike any other air on earth; their lungs filled without effort. The sun was warm. Thomas stood back and stared at his lovely woman.

'That I might drink and leave the world unseen, and with thee fade away into the forest dim,' he said. A smile came to the corner of her mouth.

'Come and kiss me!' she whispered. 'Kiss me! Kiss me!'

He held her to him as closely as he could, and kissed her hard.

'Let's do it!' her breath said. 'Let's do it! Let's lie down and do it!'

'I can't,' stammered Thomas.

'You must! You must!'

'Not with bears in the bushes.'

But there were other times when they lay down together at the lakeside, and the bears never bothered them. Florence claimed they'd made love together more times than many married couples in all their married lives.

The days passed. The trout in the fast Bow River wiggled against the current without hindrance from the airmen, who were now kept busy with valves, wires, condensers and transformers. One by one, Thomas treated his students to a flight in his little yellow aeroplane; sometimes north to Kicking Horse Pass; sometimes south to Montana.

There was a dance at the school one night. It was a pleasant night, and Thomas and Florence decided to walk home. They stopped to lean over the bridge and look into the starlit river. And then the world stopped.

It began as a gentle, ever so gentle, breeze, wafting smoothly from the west. And then there came perfume, many perfumes. The perfumes not only filled their lungs but seemed to flood their entire bodies. There was no feeling; there was neither hot nor cold. They couldn't move. They were hypnotised. The sensation was divine, out of this world. It could have lasted seconds, minutes, hours. When they returned to near normal it was painful; their bodies and souls demanded more. Their eyes looked into each other's eyes until there were only eyes. It was sexual without the physical touch.

'What's happened to us?' asked Thomas.

'We're so lucky,' she said, 'oh, so very lucky. It hasn't happened to many. I could happily have died while it lasted, like in that poem of yours.'

'So could I. I wish we had. Perhaps it was death.'

'Oh no, Tom, it wasn't death; it was life.'

'Go on.'

'What happens is that the warm air cools over the snow of the Rockies, then it sweeps down the slopes, and it's so pure that it picks up all the perfumes of the flowers on its way. But there's an Indian legend about it. Once there was a beautiful young maiden who fell in love with a warrior from another tribe. Both tribes said there could be no wedding, and the young warrior was sent far away from his people. The poor girl fretted, and soon everybody felt sorry for her; she was wasting away. And then one evening just as the first star had risen she saw a white stallion standing on the edge of the village. She dressed herself in all her blue beads and finery after she had bathed herself in the most intoxicating perfumes, and she jumped on the stallion and galloped away, calling her lover's name. They say the great Manito turned her into a spirit, and that was her just now riding the wind, still searching for her lover. It's called the Chinook. There, Tom, I know myths and legends too, and when we're married I shall tell them to our children.'

The next morning, Larry Revitt stood by the window with his gun. Sergeant Shabaga reloaded the other. Thomas stood quietly behind them; he knew better than to open his mouth when his commander was on the warpath. Bang!

'Gotcha you little varmint!' He tossed his rifle to Shabaga. 'No, don't bother passing me the loaded one. In fact, sergeant, hang up my guns.' Then he turned to Thomas. 'The gophers have won, buddy. Guess you've heard the news?'

'No.'

'The war's over. We can all go home.'

Thomas returned to the apartment heavy and low; he was on the verge of tears. Florence was crying; she'd heard the news.

'Oh, damn and blast the peace!' she shouted.

'Now I know how Paris felt when Troy fell and he had to part from Helen.'

'And to hell with your fornicating dead Greeks!' she screamed. 'They're dead. It's you and me, and we're still alive. Oh God, why couldn't the Chinook have taken us!'

They folded up into each other.

'The whole world will be happy,' he said. 'There'll be dancing in the streets. Men will be returning to their homes to pick up where they left off, and to pretend there was never a war. All except us two! Us bloody two!' He paused for a moment. 'But I'll be back, Florence my darling, my love, my sweetheart, my woman, my wife; I'll be bloody back as soon as I'm released.'

'No, not like that, Tom. Stay at home and wait for my letter. I've got to wait until my husband comes home so that I can tell him to his face about us. I can't tell him in a letter. I'm not ashamed. And I've got to make sure he's safe and sound and back home before I tell him. Trust me, darling. We'll be together, Tom, and married, and I'll make you a good wife. Please stay at home and wait for my letter. And then come quickly, for I shall need you; oh God how I shall need you!'

They travelled back to Winnipeg together, but he had to stay on the train. They swapped watches; his was gold, and hers was plain and ordinary, which he said was a guarantee that he'd be back if only to redeem his watch. They agreed to keep their watches always ticking.

'There you are, Thomas, just sit down by the fire and I'll make you some nice fried bread with some nice fried bacon and a nice fried chuckie-egg. I've had to skimp and save on my ration book to get it for you, but I knew you'd be hungry after coming all that way from Canada. And see how nice I've kept your desk polished. I polished it every Friday. And your bedroom is just how you left it. I changed and washed the sheets every fortnight. And I've got the kettle on. You'll see, Thomas, it'll be just as if you'd never been away. How do those words go in "The White Cliffs of Dover"? And Jimmy will go to sleep in his own little room again.'

'Jimmy probably didn't come from Moss Side, mom.'

'Oh, and that's another thing, Thomas. I did quite a lot of thinking all those years you were away; there was nothing else to do; and I think we should go and live in one of those nice districts you were always talking about, like Northenden.'

'I don't want to move,' said Thomas. He didn't want to say it was because this was his only known address, and that he was expecting an important letter.

'But you've always said – '

'I know what I've always said, mom; but I too have done a lot of thinking, and this, after all, is my dad's house.' He knew he'd trapped her with her own words, the very words she'd used so often to trap him.

'Mind you,' he went on, 'if you really want to move and aren't too bothered about leaving Moss Side, how about Canada?'

'Canada? The back-and-beyond? Never, Thomas! Whatever made you say that?'

It was out now; it had to come out. He told her about the woman he loved, and who loved him. He told her they were going to be married, but he held back on telling her she was already married. He said he would get a teaching job in Canada. He expected her face to show anger or bitterness; instead she smiled sweetly.

'Oh, Thomas, I've seen more of life than you. I've been through two wars. You should have been here to see for yourself. The girls, even the married ones, were forever throwing themselves at the Yanks and the Poles and the Canadians. I had to shift a Yank and some little bitch from my very doorway. There was a steady bump-bump-bump against the door, and when I went out to see what it was, it was the two of them, and I won't tell you what they were doing; I couldn't if I wanted to. And against my door. Well, it's all got to be forgiven and forgotten now. Things have got to get back to normal; pretend they never happened. What you experienced, Thomas, is what they call a war-time romance.'

What she said made him feel weak and dirty; she was spinning her web, and he could only escape when he received the strength of a letter. He went into the back-yard to smoke his pipe.

Home was even drearier than he'd feared. The mills and factories were bigger and blacker than he'd remembered them. The air was dirty and heavy. There was traffic noise in his ears all the time. For four years he had lived with big skies; never-ending skies; exciting, changing skies; and now the only bit of sky he could see from the back-yard was hemmed in with the black slates and chimneys of the crowding rooftops. Why had they done this to him? They had made him a Canadian and given him a wife and happiness; then they had snatched it all from him, taken away his uniform, and put him back on the streets of the slums. They hadn't even had the decency to let him see action, to find out for himself whether he had guts or no guts. He had been wounded. Everybody else was happy.

There was a letter from the Education Committee offering him the headmastership of several schools. It got him out of the house for an hour, for he rode his old bicycle down town to tell the education secretary there was no point in accepting the posts; he would be emigrating one of these days; he'd rather serve his time out as an ordinary schoolmaster in Ancoats. He'd also decided to apply for his part-time job again at Pauldens; he would need money to travel; there would be no more warrants. He would sink himself deep into work, and that way kill time.

When he returned home, his head was throbbing with dark depression; he wished he could crawl into the marble clock on the mantelpiece and let the cogs beat him senseless. In bed, he noticed the difference in putty around two of the twelve small windowpanes. That was all he had seen of the war in Europe. He made a black tent with his knees and curled up in the darkness.

He spent all weekend oiling and adjusting his bicycle, but it still squeaked as it had always done when he set off for school. His route should have taken him past the university; it was the shortest route. But now he took a new route. He didn't want to pass the university; he didn't want to see it, and certainly not say 'good morning' to it. The university had deliberately developed his brain and taught him things; it had been responsible for making him an instructor; it had been the cause of his present misery. The university could sulk if it liked, but he'd no wish to see its archway again.

As he approached Raglan Street, there were the strains of 'Danny Boy'. Dick Wilson, looking much older, very much older, put his violin down and dived into his cupboard for the bottle.

'And this time ye'll not be saying no to a wee snifter. Ar, sure 'tis grand to be having ye back, me fine warrior, but 'tis tomorrow ye'll be taking lessons, not today.'

Dick looked at his watch, pressed a button and a bell screeched through the eardrums. 'There ye are now, Thomas, modern technology has arrived; an electric bell. But sure 'twas put in for the air raids and not to save me old lungs on the police whistle.'

There were commands outside in the playground; there was marching in the corridor, but no teacher popped his head in the office.

'There have been changes, me laddo, and I must be putting ye wise on 'em. We're not called schoolmasters any more; we're teachers. Playtime is breaktime; lessons are periods. And scholars are pupils, would ye know? Ar, but they're still the same little snotty-nosed baggy-arsed sods they always was.'

'I take it the Battle of Hastings was still 1066?' said Thomas.

'I've not had a memo to say otherwise. But there's something else I must warn ye about.' He lowered his voice as though afraid of being overheard. 'My new bunch of teachers wear sports jackets every day of the week; every day of the week, just think of that.'

'And what do they wear on Friday?'

'Polo neck pullovers.'

'Why can't I start today, Dick? I'm here.'

'Today, me fine warrior, ye'll be catching a train and visiting Charlie Macgregor in hospital.'

'Hospital?'

'Aye, and 'tis where he'll stay for the rest of his life. He was badly wounded. And he's a major, with enough medals to sink a battleship.'

'How badly?'

'Well now, 'tis best to be preparing ye. For the poor man is totally blind, and with an arm and a leg missing.'

Thomas held out his cup for more whiskey. He felt sick.


Glory of youth glowed in his soul,
  Where is that glory now?


'Will you just listen to the man? "Over the Sea to Skye" morning, noon and night!' said the nurse. 'You can take being a Scot just too far. And I'm from Scotland myself. He's awful sorry for himself.' A doctor in a white coat patted the nurse's backside as he passed, and she winked at him. 'It's no use feeling sorry for yourself, I tell him.'

'Come in!' shouted Charlie, as Thomas gently tapped on his door and crept into his room. 'How are you, Thomas?'

'Could you smell me, Charlie?'

'I've got good hearing. I heard your voice. Well now, *caid mile failte*! Draw up a chair; make yourself at home, laddie. And how is it you've been keeping these long years? We've wandered mony a weary foot, but seas between us braid hae roared, so gie's a hand o' thine. It'll have to be me left hand.'

Before Thomas could answer, Charlie started off again. 'Braille is what they're telling me I should learn, laddie. They're going to teach me to read with my left hand. Isn't that something, eh? And no doubt play football with my left foot. I'd be no match for Genghis Khan right now, eh? And how've you been keeping?' Again before Thomas could get a word in: 'And 'tis a wee sort of message I have for you from some of your old scholars. They said for me to give their best respects the next time I saw you. Well, I'm not seeing you, but their best respects I gladly pass on.'

'That's nice,' said Thomas.

'Nice, is it?' Charlie wriggled himself so that he was sitting up. He put his only hand to his blind eyes.

'As you well know, laddie, most of your boys joined the Terriers after they'd left school. Smart lads. I believe you saw them marching once; you were hiding behind a lawn mower in Pauldens' window. Well, Thomas, let it be admitted they joined with a great deal of encouragement from me. Ach, it was something for them to do on Sunday mornings, and they went to annual camp at the beauty spots. We were the first in, and we saw plenty of beauty spots. There was the beach at Dunkirk; the first time most of them had ever seen the sea. And El Alamein, with its golden sand and palm trees.' Charlie laughed. 'The kids from Shit Creek as Dick calls them, eh? The Ancoats mob! Irish and Italian. Most of the Irish were neutral and didn't know it, and the Italians were probably fighting their uncles and cousins. But, Jesus, they fought, man! Then a piss-arsing bridge in Holland put paid to their grand tour. We were surrounded and outnumbered, and they were cutting us up like cake at a kids' party. There was only one slender chance of breaking through, and Sergeant Alker came up with it. Remember what Mavis wrote up on the blackboard, he shouted. Charge for them bleeding guns! Aye, we did at that. They were all killed. I was the unlucky one. This is me here in this bed. And seeing 'em being cut to ribbons was the last thing I saw, or ever will see. Ach, Thomas, it was marching to the band on Sunday mornings; I didna mean to lead them to their deaths. I didna think there'd be a war.'

'Was there a war?' asked Thomas, turning his sarcasm on himself.

There wasn't a great deal more to talk about. Thomas experienced the embarrassment of a sighted person talking to a blind person without reminding them of things that had once been seen, or were being seen, or ought to be seen. On Charlie's request, he promised to bring vodka in a lemonade-labelled bottle next time he visited; vodka, Charlie explained, was colourless and odourless; it would never be detected in the hospital.

The Horsfall Museum was still open when Thomas went back to Ancoats for his bike. He had to talk to somebody, and Miss

Hindshaw was exactly the right person in his mood. She was glad to see him. She looked as old and as graceful as ever; no older, for she had always been old and graceful.

'It's a blessing you're back,' she said. 'This has been a deserted museum; it will be Ancoats Hall again.'

'First find the people,' said Thomas. 'They're all dead.' He told her about Charlie.

'Here's a cup of tea,' she said.

'I've been fifteen years a teacher one way or another, and most of the boys I've taught have been killed. I'm resigning, I'm quitting, I'm getting out of it. I'm going in for commercial art where all I need to do is paint delighted ducks and merry moo-cows.'

'Mr Davies, tell me, how many Spartans survived at Thermopylae?'

'You know as well as I do – none.'

'What year was that?'

'480 BC.'

'480 BC. And after that date come Aeschylus, Sophocles, Euripides, Aristophanes, Herodotus, Xenophon, Socrates, Plato, Aristotle, Euclid, Pythagoras and Hippocrates; medicine, mathematics, science and art. And all these after Thermopylae, and maybe because of Thermopylae. But then I shouldn't be telling you this; you're the expert.' She sighed. 'I suppose some of the lads in your first classes have got young sons at your school today. You know, Mr Davies, I can never remember whether you take sugar.'


His interview with Mr Wingate was difficult. It was as if the constant procession of shop assistants had been stage managed to interrupt on cue with their queries, but they finally had a whole free minute.

'I think it can be arranged to have you back, lad,' said Mr Wingate. 'I'll just have to fill in this staff form. Now then, you've told me what you did in the war, but for your sake, it won't do.'

'Won't do?'

'Won't do. Y'see, lad, the war's over and we're all equal again. Now most of our male assistants were foot-sloggers in the poor bloody infantry, and they haven't, as you well know, a great deal of love for the Brylcream boys. White sheets to sleep between, white bread and sugar on the canteen tables, bacon and eggs when you came back from your little spins; see what I mean? And, summat else, most of our excellent male assistants were just ordinary common or garden privates and corporals. They'll hold it against you, lad. So tell me what's the lowest grade in the Air Force?'

'Aircraft Hand, Second Class, General Duties.'

'That's it then, lad; sounds good too. That's what I'll put you down as, then there'll be no jealousies or bad feeling or owt like that.' Mr Wingate started to write on the form, then stopped his pen. 'No, bugger it! I like you, lad; always did. I'll put you down as corporal.'

'Thank you,' said Thomas.

'And now let's get down to brass tacks. You'll find things a bit changed on the display side, lad. All that Teddytail, Winnie the Pooh, and Rupert the Bear crap is old-fashioned; it's finished. This is the age of the superman, super this, super that, super everything. No more cuddly little bunny rabbits; you've got to think strong. A contented cow over the meat department is out; what we want is a big burly bull beating its chest, a cunning fox peeping round a wardrobe because it's a shrewd bargain, a majestic eagle for the highest quality in town. Think big; think strong, lad. After all, we won the war.'


Morning after morning after morning was the same. His mother got up long before he did. He could hear the carpet-brush knocking against chair legs, the back-yard door opening and shutting, the tap being turned on and off; eventually the shout: 'Come on now, Thomas, your porridge is ready. Don't let it get cold.'

'Any post?' was his first question on coming down.

Sometimes she would put her arm around him and there would be a tear in her eye. 'I'm sorry, chuck. But never mind; tomorrow is another day.' But other times she would sneer: 'Why, are you expecting any?'

Little things began to upset him; he couldn't bear to hear the chimes of Big Ben on the radio. And then a big thing hurt him. Canada changed its national flag from the red one of the old dominion to a red maple leaf on a white background. This, to

Thomas, was the final rejection; Canada had given him his answer; the nation had turned him down.

'You'll not believe it, Thomas,' his mother said one morning. 'I wouldn't have believed it myself had I not seen it with my own two eyes. But there's some niggers moved in ten doors away; they're as black as the ace of spades. I don't know what your dad would have said.'

'You mean coloured people, don't you?' said Thomas.

'Call them what you will, they're not us; they're not civilised. They didn't even brownstone their steps when they moved in. And not an aspidistra in the window, oh no! Nor a pot dog, nor a cherry boy! But a packet of corn flakes.'

'They must be civilised if they eat corn flakes instead of porridge,' shouted Thomas, and he got out of the house and on his bike as quickly as he could.

Dick Wilson offered him a drink as soon as he walked in the office.

'Come on, me fine warrior, and brace yourself, for me news this morning is that 'tis the end of civilisation as we know it.'

'I've just come away from a conversation like that,' said Thomas, 'but, go on, tell me.'

''Tis this little instrument of the devil,' said Dick, and he picked a ballpoint pen up from his desk. 'The ballpoint pen. And we're to issue them out to the little sods instead of pens and nibs. The ink-wells are to be removed.'

The news hurt Thomas as though he had been stabbed with the ballpoint itself. How could the pupils possibly write Virgil out with those fine upstrokes and downstrokes? The ballpoint pen had no ambition, no discipline, no sense of beauty; nobody cared if it was lost or stolen; nobody was proud to own one. The school pen graduated to the fountain pen, and the fountain pen could have a gold clip. The ballpoint pen was anybody's harlot.

'Their writing will suffer, and they won't get the jobs,' he said.

'Ar, sure, of course they'll get the jobs; a monkey or a mongrel dog could get a job these days. This is the post-war reconstruction; there are more jobs than people; they're even bringing people in from abroad. There's jobs for everybody, me fine upstanding feller, whether they can read or write or not. Except for me.'

'What do you mean by that?'

146

'Me retirement is long overdue because of that Hitler problem, but now 'tis official. Friday's the day I go.'

'I'll be on my own, Dick.'

'Aye, so ye will; but not as much on your own as me.' He held up his bottle of whiskey. 'For I'll be parting company with me lifelong friend. Aw, Thomas, how the hell do I get me drop o' booze from time to time? There's Kitty now, and a finer woman ye couldn't wish for, and that's a fact; but, d'y'see, she thinks I'm a teetotaller. When we were first married she made me promise not to touch the stuff, and 'twas me sacred word I gave, so it was. Sure the last thing she's suspected is that I get me wee nips at school. Ar, this school has been a good pub to me, this blessed Raglan Street. 'Tis a bitter blow I'll be facing on me retirement.'

'Weedkiller,' said Thomas.

'Hold on, Thomas; not that bitter I'd want to – '

'You've a garden and a garden shed, haven't you? And the weeds'll need keeping down. A weedkiller label is all you need.'

'Thomas, ye're as crafty as a cartload o' monkeys. I can depart in peace, and face me retirement like a man. Are ye sure now, ye'd not be wanting to take over my job? Ye'll find it lonely when I'm gone, though I say it meself, for you're not one of them galoots out there.'

The galoots were the other teachers, and Thomas knew it would be lonely. Dick was right; he was not one of them, though heaven knows he'd tried. He'd continued the tradition of wearing a dark suit and dark tie from Monday to Thursday, and his old Harris tweed jacket on Friday. When other teachers had tried to bribe their pupils with sweets, or talk down to the level of the pupils in order to appear to be one of them, he had lashed them with his sarcasm; he had kept aloof, and it had worked. There had been no need for him to become the headmaster; more often than not, instead of the teacher threatening to send a rebel to the headmaster, it had been Mr Wilson who had subdued the boy by sending him to Mr Davies. But the main difference seemed to be a cultural one. Thomas's poets were Masefield, Davies, De la Mare and Robert Louis Stevenson; their one and only poet was T. S. Eliot, and their favourite poem, *The Waste Land*. He'd tried to understand *The Waste Land* in an attempt to be one of them, but it had been more like a Renaissance crossword puzzle than a modern poem, even though he was

147

able to solve some of the clues. They never turned up to see his children's theatre productions. They preferred Roman history to Greek.

On Friday afternoon the message monitor brought Thomas an invitation to join the headmaster in his office. It would be for a farewell drink.

Dick was slumped over his desk with his head in his hands. There were two large cups of whiskey on the desk. He looked sadly up at Thomas.

'I was telephoned with the news ten minutes ago,' he began. 'It was suicide. Another bloody suicide! He'd been saving his sleeping pills, then he downed them with a bottle of vodka.'

Thomas sat down shocked.

'Christ, Dick! I gave him the vodka.'

'Ar, sure not to be fretting your head, me grand feller, for didn't we all? 'Twas what he had instead of daffodils. What beats me is how he disposed of the empties? Somebody must have helped him.'

'Flora Macdonald,' said Thomas.

'Oh aye?' asked Dick.

'Wasn't she the lass who helped Bonnie Prince Charlie escape over the sea to Skye? His nurse, I'd guess.'

'Well, I'll say this now. He certainly went out with a hundred pipers an' a'. *Slainté*, Charlie!'

The two men clinked cups.

There would be loneliness without Dick, and Thomas was tempted to accept the headmastership; but he decided against it; there might some day be a letter, and he would be away. Then he sneered to himself – and Canada might go back to its old flag. Nevertheless, he made up his mind to break the silence with Florence, and he wrote her a letter. But he wrote it as though from a woman friend she'd met during the war. He made the letter general; he wrote about things in general; he said he hoped to visit Canada; he said he was lonely; he asked for a quick return letter. He signed it 'Louise'.


Four hundred pairs of eyes watched for the arrival of the new headmaster. He came in a Morris Eight and left it parked in the road. Thomas stepped out to meet him. He was a middle-aged

148

man, grey hair, red face, dark suit with white shirt and blue tie. Thomas was pleased about the dark suit.

'How d'y'do!' said the new headmaster, holding out his hand. 'Jack Hollingworth, call me Jack. And you're – '

'Thomas Davies, call me Thomas.'

'Welsh, eh?'

'I don't know; I don't honestly know.' And this was an honest answer, Thomas didn't know. He'd asked his mother when he was a small boy where she and his dad were born, and she'd told him to mind his own business and not be cheeky. He'd never enquired again.

'Well, I've heard all about you, feller,' said Jack. 'You've a bloody good reputation. Lord of Ancoats Hall, eh? I've read about your plays in the papers. Keep it up, feller! Far be it from me to interfere. You're free to use your own methods without hindrance. But sport is what we want at this school, lots of sport, lots of swimming. Cups and trophies on the walls, eh? Cricket, football, boxing, eh? Don't worry, feller, I'll handle it; just you carry on as you are doing. All I ask of you is to get involved. Parent–teacher relationship, teacher–pupil relationship, eh? Don't be aloof; get involved.' Singing came from the hall.

But of all the world's brave heroes
    There's none that can compare
With a tow-row-row-row-row-row
    To the British Grenadier.

'And that bloody noise has got to be stopped for a kick-off,' went on Jack. 'They sound like rusty circular saws or dying ducks in a thunderstorm. We'll have 'em making music, playing recorders. And I believe kids are getting interested in guitars. Used to be whip and top for us, eh?'

'What do you think of T. S. Eliot?' asked Thomas.

'Me, I'm a Rudyard Kipling man. Triumph and disaster, eh?'

With some slight misgivings, Thomas was pleased with the new headmaster; they were on the same side by the look of things.

Dick Wilson had told him that education was up against big money. There was no way he could convince his boys that in the long term it was better to start work as a humble clerk or a laboratory apprentice than grab the bulging wage packet of a bricklayer's labourer. Dick Whittington had sold his cat. The old visits to the old places could no longer inspire.

There were more half-submerged orange boxes floating on the alley-alley-o than big ships, the Ship Canal was beginning to stagnate. He had made up his mind that education from now on would be to teach his boys to spend their future big earnings on the right kind of leisure.

A little luck came his way, for if the city was losing its seaport, it was gaining an airport. The disused landing field at Ringway was being converted into what some optimistic town councillors said would become an international air terminus. There were already sufficient planes using the new runways to make an occasional visit worth while. There in the fresh Cheshire air Thomas told them about the internal combustion engine, and about the faraway places they could fly to in days to come. The bus passed through Northenden on its route to and from, and he usually looked down at the toecaps of his shoes for those five minutes. He applied to the travel offices in town for posters, and he filled the classroom walls with them.

He used the rooms of the Horsfall Museum more often than he did the school classrooms. There was an unlimited supply of pictures and objects for art classes, but his own favourite room remained the Athens Room. The bust of Homer had gone, but he still talked about Homer as though he had known him personally, although he never touched on the *Iliad* for the *Iliad* was about slaughter: instead he told them about the *Odyssey* for that was about personal adventure, with its setbacks and shipwrecks and triumphs. He would not interest his boys in warfare.

This aversion to war affected his plays at the children's theatre. No more Shakespeare with his drums and spears and swords and glory: he put on the comedies of Ben Jonson. They were done in a Laurel and Hardy slapstick style; doors fell down instead of opening, characters made funny faces at the audience when speeches got a bit dull, they laughed at Jonson's bawdiness, but then, when all was said and done, it was mild compared to the coarseness he'd overheard in the playground.

Thomas told all this to Jack while he made him an instant coffee on the gas ring. Throughout, the new headmaster nodded with agreement.

150

'And we could get 'em going to the Hallé; ram a bit of decent music in their ears till they learn to like it,' added Jack. He took his coffee to the window and looked out.

'Jesus bloody wept!' he spluttered.

'What's up?'

'My bloody Morris Eight! There's two wheels missing! It's jacked up with bricks!'

'Welcome to Ancoats,' said Thomas.


Sunday was rehearsal day. Thomas never ceased to marvel that kids who could tear each other to pieces on Saturday nights over the rival football teams of City and United could turn up the best of pals for rehearsals on Sunday mornings; and it was always a miracle they could learn such difficult and lengthy parts, although he usually cut them down to size and changed obscure words before duplicating the pages on his gelatine tray.

*Volpone* looked like becoming one of his best productions; it was pure pantomime. The idea of a rich old moneygrabber being given expensive presents by greedy toffs in the hope they'd be left a lot of money in the old man's will, and that some of the toffs were quite prepared to let their pretty young wives go to bed and have it off with Volpone for the same reason, was just the thing for the Ancoats kids. Volpone would be their hero from the start; he would be cheered to the echo.

Thomas had, from a model made on his desk at home, worked out the stage presentation. The stage was divided into two parts by a screen, and the old miser, instead of lying on a couch in front of everybody when he was pretending to be dying, would be in a separate room listening, and making all actions, doubling up with bellyache, holding his head and pretending to catch lice in his hair for a headache, hopping about on one foot for a poorly toe. Volpone would also peep round the screen to see what presents the toffs had brought him, then pretend to count his wealth on his fingers and rub his hands with delight. All the cast were to be dressed as clowns, and when the action was in Volpone's bed-room, his pals in the main room would play pitch and toss in silence. Alker was Volpone, and he was perfect. Tears came to Thomas's eyes with Alker's antics. Alker's father, Thomas remembered, had been a good actor, but the son was better; he

151

threw in ad libs like a pepperpot.

He wore Thomas's old cap and gown for the quack medicine man's auction of his bottles of wonder cure.

'These here bottles have the complete cure for guts ache, fin rot, mange, distemper, bad eyesight, pains in the backside, stuffed nose, wax in the ear, chilblains and Crewe Junction. I'm not asking five pounds, four pounds, one pound, ten shillings; all I'm asking is one penny.'

Thomas guessed there would be bids from the audience; Alker was as persuasive as any Tib Street quack.

'We will eat at such a meal, the heads of parrots, tongues of nightingales, the brains of peacocks and of ostriches,' were Ben Jonson's lines. 'But give me sixpennorth of fish and chips,' added Alker.

When Lady Politick Would-be offered to cure the old codger's ailments with some English saffron, sixteen cloves, syrup of apples, tincture of gold, a little musk, dried mint and barley-meal, he sat up on his couch like a jack-in-the-box and recited:

Beechams pills cure all ills
    A penny a box gets rid of pox.

Thomas was troubled with the final scene, the magistrate's court, for, nailed above the magistrate's chair was a large coat of arms; there was no doubt it was the real thing, and the only possible explanation was that it had been stolen from the city magistrate's court, but he couldn't see how his boys, even his boys, could get away with such a theft.

One of the boys had borrowed his father's record player and the record of Glenn Miller's 'Little Brown Jug'. Thomas objected to it at first; he couldn't tell himself why; but it was insisted upon by the cast, and 'Little Brown Jug' was used to open the play, and in between acts.

After the boys had gone home singing 'Little Brown Jug' on their way, Thomas sat in Miss Hindshaw's office, supping tea and chatting until the September sky grew grey. It was dark by the time he'd cycled through Ardwick, but the sky was lit up with a fitful red glow on the town side of the university, in the All Saints direction. He was compelled out of curiosity to cycle

152

towards the glow.

The whole building of Pauldens was burning like a torch; flames were dancing into the sky. There was fire engine after fire engine, and ladders were swivelling and extending towards the burning building; the flames reflected in the brass helmets of a hundred firemen; there were jets of water in all directions; flames licked out from every window. Thomas joined the thousand people who were pushing as near as the police cordon would allow. He stared, and could feel the heat on his face.

'Just like the bloody blitz, isn't it?' said a woman next to him. Thomas didn't answer.

Suddenly the corner dome, which had always given the store the appearance of a college, swayed and toppled into the centre of the fire. A shower of sparks like fireworks crackled higher than the flames for a second.

'I said just like the bloody blitz,' the woman repeated.

The entire frontage rumbled and dropped into the fire; the flames subsided for a few moments, then the cascade of sparks spread higher than ever.

The woman elbowed Thomas. 'Bloody ignorant sod, aren't you?' she snarled. 'I said it was just like the bloody blitz.'

'I didn't see the bloody blitz,' shouted Thomas. 'I couldn't get tickets.' He nudged his way to the back of the building; it was where his stable studio was; there might be a possibility that some of his cut-outs could have fallen into the side street.

As he stood in the black smoke, four figures silhouetted by the flames came out of the building carrying a coffin. No, it wasn't a coffin, it was a wardrobe. The heat draught blew the wardrobe door open and he could see it was filled with pots and pans. One of the figures shut the wardrobe door and the group trundled on. Thomas could see they were boys from his school. Another boy came out of the building; he was patting his hair because it was singed; he carried a bulging pillowcase which tinkled as though full of crockery. And then another lad stumbled out; he carried an enamel bowl filled to the brim with clocks and artificial jewellery. Various pieces of the jewellery fell in the street. Thomas impulsively picked them up and stuffed them in his pocket. He knew the boys. They got lost in the darkness; nobody noticed them; the great fire was the only attraction. Thomas got on his bike and cycled to the nearest pub; there was something he had to think about, and he desperately needed a pint of beer to wash his thoughts down.

The boys were looters, there was no doubt about that. His duty was to give their names to the police. But were they looting or just salvaging? After all, everything in the store was being burnt to ashes. Had they not helped themselves to those commodities, those commodities would be destroyed. And if he handed over their names, they would be sent to a Borstal institution, and that would help nobody. Besides, one of the boys was Alker, and he was the perfect Volpone.

His mother was waiting at the front door. She was trembling. 'Oh, Thomas, thank God you're alive. I heard the news on the wireless, and I was afraid you might have been inside because you do turn in on Sundays sometimes. I knelt down and prayed to God that you would be safe.'

Thomas put his arm round her and helped her into the house. She stopped trembling.

'I'll make you a nice cup of coffee and chicory,' she said, and fumbled off into the scullery. Thomas seized the opportunity to empty his pockets and put the artificial jewellery in his desk drawer and lock it.

'It was a hundred years old, Pauldens was,' came her voice from the scullery. 'They said it might have been the first department store of its kind in the world. There were twenty fire engines and five turntable ladders, the man said. And he said a rough estimate of the damage was two million pounds. And I kept thinking of you while he was talking.'

She came out of the scullery with his cup of coffee; her face had brightened, she was smiling.

'But let's look on the bright side,' she said. 'You'll be able to spend Saturdays with me from now on.'


But come ye back when summer's in the meadow,
   Or when the valley's hushed and white with snow;
'Tis I'll be here in sunshine or in shadow;
   O Danny Boy! O Danny Boy! I love you so.


The thick dark red curtains closed noiselessly around the coffin, and Thomas led Kitty out of the crematorium and into the

Rolls Royce.

'Here,' she said when they were back in the house. 'You could maybe do with a drop of this.' She poured out a glass of whiskey from a bottle labelled 'Poison. Weedkiller'. 'I found it down in the garden shed.' She gave a little laugh. 'He thought I didn't know, but I knew, though I never let on I knew.'

'He told me he made a promise,' said Thomas.

'Oh, indeed he did; when we were first married. And he kept to it. "Kitty, me darling," he said at the time, "I promise ye'll never see me touch a drop of the hard stuff again till death do us part." And sure I never saw him put a glass to his lips. He enjoyed his school drinking; 'twas the secret of it, y'know. It would have spoiled things for him if he'd known I knew. But couldn't I smell it on his breath even with the peppermints?'

'I'll miss him.'

'We all will, Thomas.' She looked proud. 'And we've a wonderful family. 'Tis a pity you never got married and had a family. The elder boy's at Oxford and wants to be a teacher. The other lad's mad to go on the stage. And our daughter's married to a doctor. Now isn't that something! But I'm glad they didn't come back with us. Dick would have preferred you to have a last quiet nip of his weedkiller. He thought a lot of you, Thomas. "'Tis proud I am to be supporting that man with his gallivanting ways of education," he would say. "It's our job to protect him."'

'Protect me? Against what?'

'Against the outside,' she said. It was clear she intended to say nothing more on the subject. She picked up his violin case.

'I shall be going back to Ireland to stay with my sister. I'll maybe give this old fiddle to a street beggar to earn a few coppers with.'

Thomas decided to risk a small joke. 'And tell him, Kitty, the old fiddle will play "Danny Boy" on its own while he goes round with the hat.'

Kitty's eyes sprang into great tears; she made a loud wailing groan, and buried her face in Thomas's coat.


'Tell you what, feller,' said Jack, sticking his chin forward. He had a square chin and a habit of pushing it towards Thomas, which Thomas imagined Bulldog Drummond would do. 'Best thing you ever did was put me on to Honest Amy over those tyres. She sold them back to me at a fraction of what they'd have cost if I'd had to buy new ones.'

'I told you she would. She's very honest.'

'And I've been popping into her shop every week for little odds and ends. She's got a gold mine and doesn't know it. Some of her stuff is practically antique. The wife and I went for a mooch around on Saturday, and there in a corner, covered over in old curtains and carpets – it'd been there for years and Amy had forgotten it – was an old-fashioned gramophone, one of those with the big horn, remember?'

'Green.'

'That's right, a large green horn. And a stack of old wax records, those with the dog on.'

'Of military marches.'

'That's right. "How much?" I said. "Make me an offer," she said. Hey, feller, how did you know?'

'Guessed,' said Thomas.

'"Two quid," I said. "Done," she said. Well, I'm telling you, feller, we put it in the car and drove straight down to an antique shop in Saint Anne's Square and flogged it for a fiver. How's that, eh? Oh, I dare say Honest Amy thought she was pulling a fast one on me over those tyres, but I sized her shop up, and I've made a few quid profit out of her since. Not bad, eh?'

'Is that your sideline? Dabbling in antiques?'

'No, feller, that's my hobby. Buying old boneshakers and doing 'em up into decent motor cars is my sideline. It's what gives the wife and I a holiday in Italy every year.'

Mention of Italy reminded Thomas about something which was worrying him; although the country concerned was Holland. He had started school trips abroad; boys paid small amounts each Monday into the fund. Thomas banked the money and kept the accounts, but never went on any of the trips even though accompanying teachers could go free. Canada had betrayed him by changing their flag, but he wasn't going to betray Canada by going to any other country. In any case, there were always volunteers from the young T. S. Eliot teachers. What Thomas did do while they were away was study all about the country they'd gone to in the Central Library so that he could question them on their return. The Central Library was the same thing as Paris, Rome

156

or Copenhagen. The coming holiday, the library would be Amsterdam, for the trip was to Holland. There was a boy who had paid his pound every Monday, then disappeared and was absent from school for the rest of the week, and this had happened for a couple of weeks. What was happening? He told Jack his problem.

'Like I've told you, feller; get involved. Go round to the house, knock on the door, and find out, eh?'

The street had once been a street of linnets; now there was a budgerigar in a cage in most windows. A man was standing outside the house.

'Join the queue,' said the man.

'Yes, right.'

'Bit like Alexandria after pay parade.'

Thomas looked up and down the dirty street with the derelict mills in the background. All he knew about Alexandria was that it had once possessed the finest library in the world with all the plays of Aeschylus before they were lost for ever. It was near the Pharos lighthouse. He couldn't see any relationship.

'In the Forces, was you?' asked the man.

'Er . . . no.' It was the easiest answer.

'Didn't miss much.'

Another man came out of the house. 'Next for shaving,' he said to Thomas's man.

'Won't be long,' the man said to Thomas as he grabbed the doorknob and walked into the house.

Thomas waited on his own, wondering what sort of reception he was going to get. One or two people passed him. They stepped to the other side of the street and stared at him, even turning round to stare at him. The man eventually came out again.

'Up she comes and the colour's red,' he said, giving Thomas a nudge and a wink. Thomas knocked and let himself in. The woman was naked except for a piece of curtain around her waist.

'Let's see the colour of your money,' she said. 'Five bob on the table.'

'I'm your son's teacher,' stammered Thomas.

'I don't give a bugger if you're his Holiness the Pope; it's five bob.' She tapped the table. 'On there.'

He put two half-crowns on the table.

'There's a misunderstanding,' he said. 'I've just called to ask why your lad hasn't been coming to school.'

'What you bloody talking about? He never misses.'

'He's missed three weeks. He comes in on Monday morning to pay his money for Holland, and that's the last we see of him.'

'Holland? I don't know what you're bloody talking about. You've got the wrong house.'

'No, I haven't.'

'Look,' she said. 'Go and sort it out with him. He's in the shit-house in the back yard. I make him stay out there when callers come. Then come back and tell me what it's all about, I'd like to bloody know.' She flopped down on a sofa and flicked a lighter to a cigarette.

Thomas had to unbolt the scullery door; the lad had been locked out. He found him smoking a cigarette on the lavatory.

'You've come to ask why I've not been at school, haven't you, sir?'

'That just about sums it up.'

'Well, it's cos I want to go to Holland.' The boy took a deep drag on his cigarette.

'Missing school won't get you to Holland; it'll only get you across the river to the reform school.'

'I help a feller on his coal round, sir. He gives me a quid for a week's work, and lets me wash before coming home.'

'And the quid is for Holland?'

'Yes, sir.'

'Why?'

'Cos I want to go to Holland, sir.'

'Why?'

'Cos they wear wooden clogs and have windmills and it's where the boy stuck his finger in the dyke and it's where me dad was killed.' He dropped the cigarette end between his legs, and it hissed in the lavatory water.

'I know about your dad and Holland,' said Thomas. 'I'll go back and talk to your mother.'

'And will you ask her if I can come in now? It's getting cold.'

His mother had switched the radio on.

The holly and the ivy,
   When they are both full grown,

158

'Oh, Thomas, sometimes I think you're very cruel to me. Why can't we move to a nice district with privet hedges, just for the remainder of my days? I haven't many days ahead of me. The doctor told me to take care, and, Thomas, I've lived such a lonely life. And Moss Side is filling up with niggers everywhere you turn.'

'I'm not leaving my dad's house,' said Thomas. He knew he was being cruel to his mother, but then she had been cruel to him; she kept him like a canary in a cage in a warm room. She would only ever take ten shillings towards his keep, and the very suggestion they should try some of the new foods on the market would be enough to send her slamming cupboard doors. 'I do my best on the little you give me, but of course if you don't think I'm looking after you properly you can always go somewhere else,' was her stock reply.

She seemed to read his mind, for whenever he felt compelled to run out of the house and never come back, she would sniffle: 'You're all I've got in life, chuckie, and I'm all you've got. And there's your dad looking down on us, and sometimes I imagine I see him smile.' Thomas blushed at his instinct to throw a shoe at the photograph; it nauseated him to see his mother, an old woman with gnarled hands and blue veins, pointing up to the picture of a young man; it seemed obscene, and he too felt embarrassed in a shivery sort of way at pretending to look with reverence at a portrait when he was old enough to be that portrait's father. 'But I won't burden you much longer,' was her tried and trusted epilogue.

Apart from the small terraced house in which he lived, most of the buildings, decaying and rotten, were large and Georgian. They had plenty of rooms which women could rent by the night. With money coming down like snow all over Britain, the cheap whores of the knocking shops were superseded by ladies who travelled down by taxi from their swanky apartments in the better part of town. Men had money, and the going rate for sex made it a paying proposition. The prostitutes paraded the roads, the whores plied their trade down the back streets.

Thomas sat at his desk all day on Saturday with his view of the dustbin and the lavatory door, and Thomas Davies read Thomas

De Quincey, for apart from their first names, he felt they had a lot in common. De Quincey had been born and had spent the early years of his life in one of the big houses just a few streets away in Greenheys Lane; his father had died when he was young; he had been brought up by his mother. But it was De Quincey's words which tumbled into Thomas's brain; he spoke of barrel organs and Babylon, Luther and Levana; and he had written 'Her face was the same as when I saw it last, and yet again how different! Seventeen years ago, when the lamp-light fell upon her face, as for the last time I kissed her lips, her eyes were streaming with tears: the tears were now wiped away; she seemed more beautiful than she was at that time, but in all other points the same, and not older. Her looks were tranquil, but with unusual solemnity of expression, and I now gazed upon her with some awe, but suddenly her countenance grew dim, and, turning to the mountains, I perceived vapours rolling between us; in a moment, all had vanished; thick darkness came on.'

It was how De Quincey had dreamed such dreams which fascinated Thomas. Opium! Something which would take his mind from the depression in which he lived, and the squalor in which he taught; which would send the caryatids dancing in rhythm; which would fill the great dome of the Central Library with all the characters he had ever read about; Mark Antony boasting to Tom Sawyer, Aeschylus arguing with George Bernard Shaw, Ben Jonson offering everybody claret. And through these images came a stronger image of Donald Duck singing 'The Three Caballeros'.

On Saturday nights, the letter with the lipstick in his back pocket propelled him to the back streets to find a whore. His pay, now without Pauldens' extra money, and minus the money he paid for bus fares for his pupils' outings, was only enough for a back street girl.

Watching a young woman take off her clothes was good; seeing her naked was good; having intercourse was smooth and sweet. And it wasn't really real! No names were asked for or given. Nobody had to fall in love. No promises expected; no weeping farewells, just a ta-rar!

Whores? No; to Thomas they weren't whores; they were priestesses of Aphrodite. A girl could be Helen of Troy, Salome, Cleopatra, Queen Dido or Jezebel. It was physical imagination, that was all. He usually presented them with a trinket of artificial jewellery from his desk.

He was attracted by a young Jamaican girl. She shone with beauty. She was Pocahontas.

'Why you name me Pocahontas? Ain't ma name, man.'

'She was a Red Indian.'

'I'm West Indian. Okay?'

'She had a dark smooth skin.'

'If you say so. Okay.'

'She came all the way to England from across the wide Atlantic.'

'I do that. Okay.'

'She was a beautiful princess.'

'Oh, man, that very definitely me,' she laughed.

He put a silver chain around her neck; the medallion, which fell between her breasts, was of two triangles forming a six-pointed star.

'What's more, she saved a white man from getting stoned out of his mind. With Captain Smith it was a big rock; with me it could have been a small drug.'

Her body was cool; her lips were sweet; they were small lips. Her eyes were soft and brown. Her breasts were large, and her nipples pointed upwards; the medallion slid from breast to breast. Everything about her was silky. Making love to her was an anaesthetic; he could lose himself in movement. She was a young girl; sometimes it worried him that he was becoming old with grey hair. Was it similar to his old mother looking up at the portrait of her young husband? It didn't matter. Pocahontas told him she loved him; he knew she couldn't mean it, but it was wonderful just to be lied to.


The timetable in the headmaster's office had never changed over the years. Friday still said 'Scripture', and Friday therefore was always a free day for Thomas to do what he liked with his school-leaver class. He marched them out early one Friday morning.

'Where you taking them today?' asked Jack. 'To join the Foreign Legion?'

'Jodrell Bank,' said Thomas. 'We'll catch the train to Alderley Edge and walk the rest of the way. Do 'em good!'

'Do 'em better if they went to the swimming baths instead,' said Jack a little morosely. There had been a difference of opinion between the two men. Jack Hollingworth thought that Thomas's trips came under the heading of 'gadding about' when the pupils would be better employed at sport, and in particular swimming; there was a swimming gala coming up for an inter-school shield, and there were one or two promising lads in Thomas's class who might possibly win that shield for the school wall, but the lads needed all the swimming practice they could get.

The class stood in the field by the giant radio telescope with its immense two hundred and fifty foot diameter saucer looking up at the sky.

Oh! I have slipped the surly bonds of earth ...
    Put out my hand
And touched the face of God.

He was pleased that all of his class had roughly remembered the poem he'd set them; a learnt poem was still his price of admission to any of his gadding-abouts. He told them that Bernard Lovell had put the telescope together from bits and pieces of wartime radio surplus equipment, and that it had all been done at the university down the road. He was still not talking to his university, and he refused to give it the proper title.

Thomas knew what he was talking about, for he had taught himself all about it many years ago. It began, he told them, with a little gadget in the tail of an aeroplane called IFF, which meant 'Identification Friend or Foe', then it was called radar: today, he went on, this great achievement of the place down the road is in touch with every star in the sky; it sent up signals and bounced them off the stars and planets; it tracked space rockets for the Americans and Russians.

'I don't know why you're telling us this, sir. They're never going to send a kid from Ancoats up into space,' said a voice.

'They might,' added another voice, 'when they run short of dogs and monkeys.'

'I'm telling you to get you interested in modern science,' said Thomas. 'To give you pride in your city. Today there are no limits. *Arduus ad Solem.*'

'What's that mean, sir?'

'It means that with effort you can reach the sun.'

'Aye, and get your bloody fingers burnt.'

'Like Diddy Daylus, sir. He got his bum burnt.'

Thomas was pleased that O'Brien had remembered one of his stories from the Athens Room.

'That was mythology, O'Brien. The stars used to be mythology. Later, the shapes they made in the sky became guides to the old-fashioned navigators. Today the stars are realities. Science brings them nearer every year. Some day we shall go to the planets.'

'Can we go next Friday, sir? If I pay me own bus fare?'

'Please, sir, d'y'think Jodrell Bank will ever bounce a signal off God's bum?'

Thomas decided to answer a facetious question with a serious reply.

'It is probably doing that already,' he said. 'It's just that we don't know who or what God is.'

After the inevitable prologue of jokes, the class settled down, and Thomas was gratified to feel they were interested; they stopped nudging each other and giggling; they were absorbed. And they remained interested until it was time to march off down the long hill to Alderley Edge. A scuffling began; a running, chasing and throwing. The boys began to pelt each other with pats of cow dung from the field they were in. Their skin, hair and clothes became covered in putrid stinking dung. They looked more like chocolate soldiers by the time Thomas managed to get them out on the road.

At Alderley station, the porter sent for the foreman, and the foreman sent for the stationmaster.

'There's no way I'm going to let them lads on any of my trains,' said the stationmaster. 'My trains come from London with Londoners. What the bloody hell are they going to think of Manchester? And the next bloody stop is Wilmslow, and they're posh people in Wilmslow. They'll never travel by train again.'

'But I've got to get them back to Ancoats,' Thomas begged.

'Aye, well you shoulda thought of that before you started teaching 'em to throw shit at each other.'

The stationmaster eventually allowed Thomas to use his telephone, and he phoned Jack with his problem. Jack promised to do something as quickly as possible, and an hour later two open trucks arrived, boldly painted 'Manchester Corporation Cemeteries Dept'.

The trucks had to slow down with the traffic as they approached Wilmslow, and Thomas felt like a marquis on a tumbril during the French Revolution; he guessed what might happen in Wilmslow.

'We are the champions!' shouted the boys, banging their fists against the truck sides. People stood on the pavements and watched.

'It was the good ship Venus, my God you should have seen us!'

'Cats on the rooftops, cats on the tiles!'

'Here, missus, have a bit of Mars. It's where we've just come from,' shouted one of the boys, scooping dung from his jacket and throwing it at a lady with a poodle.

The trucks did not go to Raglan Street; they'd been instructed to drive to New Islington public baths, where Jack was waiting for them with a rolled towel under his arm.

'Right, lads, straight under the showers, then into the plunge!' he ordered. 'Thanks for your co-operation, feller,' he said to Thomas, with a broad smile on his face and his jaw further forward than ever. 'Just what they needed, a bit of swimming practice. They mightn't win races, but they'll come out clean. What happened?'

'All my fault,' said Thomas. 'I made them learn the wrong poem. It should have been Gray's "Elegy" – the lowing herd winds slowly o'er the lea.'

Jack asked Thomas to go back and mind the shop for the last hour while he helped the lads improve their breaststroke. Thomas was glad of the spare hour; he had two references to write for a couple of lads who had more or less clinched their jobs subject to a good reference; one as a laboratory assistant at the Christie Hospital, the other as junior trainee in the display department of Lewis's department store. He intended to write the references in his best handwriting with specially selected adjectives.

There was the honk-honk of a taxi cab as he blotted his signature on the last letter. Pocahontas in all her colourful glory stepped out of the cab; she wore a yellow blouse and a red skirt and a broad hat of many-coloured flowers. She wore high-

166

heeled shoes with tiny chains around her ankles. She strutted into the office like a queen, but her face was sad.

'Come with me,' she said. 'I got taxi. I pay taxi man. Sammy your neighbour came and told me. Sammy your neighbour know where I live. Sammy hear bang and scream. Sammy break door down. Your mamma fallen off chair. Sammy send for ambulanceman. Sammy make her comfortable and talk a lot to her. Your mamma, she is dead and done for.'

# When he frowned

For the first time, rice was used in Thomas's house for something other than rice pudding; it was used with sauces and spices for meat and fish; it was fried in a frying pan. Pocahontas moved in with him. But she insisted on keeping her rented room for her night business. She disappeared for two or three hours every evening, and Thomas pretended to be philosophical about it. 'I suppose everybody needs a sideline,' he said. 'Just as long as you come home and tell me you love me.' She insisted on buying the food with the money which came into her large white shoulder handbag.

Sammy and his wife Stella, from the same part of Jamaica as Pocahontas, often came to tea.

'I gotta nice house and I gotta good marriage, and I go to work clean railway carriage,' said Sammy, clicking his fingers to the rhythm. 'That a shooting star come from afar? No, that a railway train been cleaned with a shammy, and done by the hand of Kingston Sammy.' He stopped clicking. 'And thanks to Tommy the teacher what wrote me a reference.'

Thomas had become involved with the West Indian Community Centre in Moss Side. It was blackboard work; he taught English language and English customs; he did his best to tell them of English prejudices and their own prejudices; he told them what jobs were going in the newspaper; he told them the manner in which to apply; he wrote references. That was on Monday nights. On Saturday nights he went to hear the steel drum band playing 'Yellow Bird on the Banana Tree'. They were always short of money for the centre, and Thomas proposed a jumble sale.

Pocahontas was given the job of sorting through his mother's belongings for the jumble sale. Thomas started the collection with the picture of his father.

'Hey, Tommy, who going to buy a big picture of a white man

168

in officer's uniform round here?' asked Pocahontas.

'The frame's worth a bob or two. And I'm sure dad would have loved to help a West Indian centre.'

She came running downstairs half an hour later with a shoe box full of jewellery which she'd found on top of the wardrobe. His mother had been standing on a chair to reach the top of the wardrobe when she had slipped. They were real jewels.

'They're yours,' said Thomas.

'Oh, no!' said Pocahontas, backing away from them as though they were evil voodoo.

'You're a princess. It's about time you had some crown jewels. Can you see me wearing them? And I'd feel guilty selling them.'

'You feel guilty, Tommy? How about me? Nigger girl steal white lady's jewels, eh? They'd put me in the lock-up, man, ain't no doubt.'

'Then I'll sign them over to you as a deed of gift through a solicitor and make it legal. No argument!'

'But I've nowhere to pin the brooches.' She was naked.

'Then put the diamond ear-rings on.'

The next job, an hour later, was to stack his mother's books for the jumble sale, but Pocahontas refused.

'I read them first,' she said. 'I like your mother's books; they all love books; they all got happy endings. I know cos I read the back pages.'

'In that case you've got about forty happy endings ahead of you.'

Thomas tried to persuade her to go with him to the rehearsals at his children's theatre, but her answer was always no. She preferred him to tell her about them when he came home.

He was rehearsing *Pinocchio* with an all-Italian kid cast and plenty of Italian music. As it was nearing Christmas, he added the *George and Dragon* mummers' play as a curtain closer. It had Saint George, the Dragon, Father Christmas, the Doctor, the King of Egypt, a Turkish Knight, and the Giant Turpin. He knew the Dragon and Giant Turpin would be cheered on the night, short though their parts were. It was only a tiny Christmas card of a play, and it would be great coming after the comedy of *Pinocchio*; it also gave him a chance to see his cap and gown on the Doctor, even though his gown was now old and torn and stained.

The Dragon, with a head made by Miss Hindshaw, killed

169

Saint George, and Father Christmas stepped to the front of the stage.

> Is there a doctor to be found
>> All ready near at hand,
> To cure a deep and deadly wound,
>> And make the champion stand?

'Please, sir,' Saint George asked Thomas, 'is it true that you once gave a man a deadly wound on the museum steps?'

For a second, Thomas was stunned.

'It is not true,' he stammered. 'The truth is I killed a kid for standing on stage and asking a daft question. Carry on!'

The Doctor stepped forward in Thomas's mortarboard, which, being too big for him, wobbled as he spoke.

> I cure diseases, whatever you pleases;
>> Consumption, the palsy, the gout.
> If the devil's in, I'll blow him out!

Thomas joined Miss Hindshaw in her office for a cup of tea.

'I shall be retiring the day after your play goes on,' she told him sweetly. 'Do you know, Mr Davies, I can never remember whether you take sugar or not.'

'Retiring? You can't!'

'Why ever not? I'm an old lady. I'm tired. Besides, you must have heard the news.'

'What news?'

'There's a demolition order on Ancoats Hall and the children's theatre. They're going to bulldoze it all down. Ah, I remember now, no sugar.'


Thomas spent hours at his desk writing letter after letter in protest against the destruction of Ancoats Hall. He wrote to the local clergymen; he wrote to his Member of Parliament; he wrote to every name in the town hall. It was, he argued, a true Elizabethan manor house in perfect proportion; cleaned up it would be beautiful. If, as they said, they were going to rebuild Ancoats, it would be an ideal community centre, a centre for the arts. If they were going to turn the area into a park, then it would add grace and dignity to the lawns and shrubs. To all his letters he received sympathetic replies. But there came one letter handwritten in flourishing roundhand. It began: 'Dear Sir, I don't suppose you remember me – ' He waved the letter with annoyance.

'Don't suppose you remember me! Don't suppose you remember me! That's what everybody says when they meet me. Of course I remember. I'm trained to remember. I remember Boadicea, Julius Caesar, William the Conqueror, Robert Bruce, Wat Tyler, Thomas More – '

'Take it easy, Tommy. Easy, easy, easy, man!' said Pocahontas.

'I remember every name on every register I've ever called. I remember the first register on my first day from Alker to Zammitt, that's how well I remember.'

'Hey, Tommy, you blow top. Read your letter, eh?'

He read on. 'But I was one of your scholars. You taught me to write for a job, and you wrote me a reference, and I started work as a clerk in a small firm of printers. I went to night school and I became manager. And now I own the business and it is expanding. So if ever you want business cards or letter-headings done at cost price, come to me.

'Your lessons in the Athens Room, particularly about democracy, interested me in local politics, and I've been a councillor for many years, elected and accountable to the people, like you used to preach. As a matter of fact, I took my wife and family for a holiday in Greece, and we saw the real things, and I was able to tell them about everything about them.

'But the reason I am writing is to tell you that I was the councillor who led the move to demolish the Horsfall Museum.

'It would be a beautiful building if done up, but nobody would ever go there, it is off the beaten track. We had a survey done, and I'm afraid the soot and chemicals over a hundred years have eaten into it like a cancer. It would take an enormous amount of money to have restored and preserved, and we need the money for other things. We are building housing estates for the working classes, and they have inside bathrooms and lavatories, no more shivering in the back-yard on a cold winter's night. And they have front lawns and back gardens, and there are trees in the avenues. The new schools have large windows, the playgrounds are lined with trees, and each school will have a large hall with a

171

stage. Aren't all these things the very things you taught us we should work for on those Fridays in Ancoats Hall, sir? And to help us to get them we must now sacrifice Ancoats Hall. The ancient Greeks would have done the same.

'By the way, sir, I know you can keep a secret. It is rumoured that in a year or two I may become Lord Mayor of Manchester, and you must take a lot of the credit for it.'

Thomas put the letter on the table. Tears of pride came into his eyes. 'Hey, daftie!' said Pocahontas, and she wiped them with her handkerchief.

'He writes a good letter,' said Thomas.

'Why not?' she said. 'He says himself you taught him.'

'Lord Mayor of Manchester, eh? Ah well, for that they can have Ancoats Hall.'

'Oh, you old daftie,' said Pocahontas. 'Everything bad that happens to you has to be a victory, else it would be a defeat. I get you glass of rum.' She pretended to tap him over the head with one of his mother's books which she'd been reading. A thin blue letter wafted out and zigzagged to the carpet. 'This one mighty big day for letters,' she laughed. Thomas knew.

'Read it to me?' he asked.

'Sure. I read.' She picked up the letter, it was an airmail letter from Canada; she opened it and read it.

' "Darling, I shall not write until I hear from you. What happened? What went wrong? When I got your letter signed Louise, I knew it was okay for me to write, so I wrote. I told you my husband had been killed in the invasion, and I told you about the baby, and I begged you to come to me. Thomas, how I needed you. I wondered if it was my husband's death which had given you a conscience or something. Or perhaps it was just a wartime romance between us and you had found another girl. Maybe you didn't want the baby, I don't know. I still love you, and whatever has happened to make you change your mind I shall always love you. The baby was born a month ago. I've called him Thomas, I hope you don't mind. I guess it was the night of the Chinook. Goodbye, and all my aching love. Florence." ' Pocahontas read the front of the letter. 'It come many year ago,' she said. 'Long time ago. I get you big glass rum, Tommy.'

When she turned round after pouring out two drinks, he was crying; sobbing quietly like a small boy who has been told his dad

172

had died.

'What you do?'

'Find her.'

'You still love her?'

'Yes.'

'Okay, so you don't love me. Maybe I don't love you. Maybe I slip away with the trade winds some fine day. I go now I think.'

'Please don't go.'

'So you want me stay protect you till you find her? Your mother protect you too much. Maybe you should not have let her protect you, Tommy. Maybe you find her, and so? But that lady no longer slip of girl like me, like when you knew her, oh no, man! She got grey hair too. Maybe fat. Maybe you could pass each other in the market and not know each other. But find her; you gotta find her! Maybe I stay and protect you because you give me jewels.'

'We waited for each other. All those years we waited for each other.'

'Meanwhile you shack up with Jamaican girl. Was you being true, Tommy?'

'In my fashion, Cynara.'

'Cynara now is it? That why you call me Pocahontas? Everything okay long as it make-believe? Okay, fine, okay! So you write your letter while I go out on my sideline, Mister Columbus.'

Thomas wrote letter after letter; the ink blots on his desk from the letters about Ancoats Hall were joined by ink blots from his letters to Fort Garry. If he finished a letter in the middle of the night, he cycled down to the General Post Office to post it. Pocahontas was always waiting to make him coffee.

He filled his letters with stories about his school, his boys, his lessons. He copied out the love poems of John Donne. He even filled one letter with a detailed explanation of how the internal combustion engine worked. He had to write, write, write. Every letter was sent by airmail, and if he heard jet engines whining over the city he imagined he was navigating the aircraft to Winnipeg by the stars. Often he cycled to the swing bridge over the Ship Canal and leaned over the rail to look west. There were no ships on the Canal, only rainbow-coloured shapes of oil slowly drifting. He sniffed the air, but the Chinook never came; instead, the sulphurous stink from the Imperial Chemical Industries

173

plant down the Canal. He usually came home from these trips cold and shivery, and Pocahontas put rum in his coffee.

No letters came back, and in despair Thomas wrote to Mo Conkergood care of the Hudson's Bay Company Store; he may have retired, but somebody might forward the letter. He told Mo everything, and asked if he would call at Fort Garry. There was a reply.

'Goddamm it, I said to my wife. This letter from England is from the Manitoba Kid. Believe me, Kid, I didn't find out until after you'd left that you were a big shot Air Force officer, and me kicking you around. I found out from a Mrs Samuels – you wouldn't know her, and the poor lady has passed away. I guess you went back to England and won the war. God, when I saw them films about what they did to my people in Belsen and Buchenwald I was sure glad I'd known a guy who'd done something about it. They wouldn't take me because of my heart, and yet here am I playing baseball with my grandchildren.

'Well, Manitoba, I did like you asked, and the news ain't good. Truth is there ain't no news. The lady left Fort Garry about a year ago. They tell me she was a very nice person who kept herself to herself. They said she seemed lonely, and spent a lot of her time down at the railroad depot just watching for the westbound trains to come in. She had a baby shortly after the war ended, a boy. Last year he graduated from McGill, and they reckon he went off to be a teacher. Then the lady herself vamoosed, and ain't ever been back. The janitor showed me a stack of mail in your handwriting. He promised to keep them in his cupboard in case she ever returns.'

Thomas knew it was finished; he stopped writing. Sometimes he walked to Platt Fields and sat on his own by the lake and watched the ducks. He was afraid of raising his eyes higher for fear there would be no glacier. He once spoke some lines by Sappho out loud.

The moon is set, and the Pleiads;
   Midnight goes by;
The hours pass onward;
   Lonely I lie.

A woman grabbed her little girl by the hand. 'Come away from that old man, Caroline. He's a bit simple.'

Thomas came home one night later than usual. He and Jack had taken about fifty boys to see *Julius Caesar* at the Opera House and they'd stopped for a few drinks, mainly because Jack wished to celebrate the school's winning of the swimming shield.

His door was open; it had been broken open. Inside, everything had been smashed; everything except his desk; somebody had left their excreta on top of it. There were daubs of excreta over the wallpaper. He felt sick. He rushed upstairs to see what they'd done there.

Pocahontas was lying naked on his bed. Her legs were apart; one knee hung over the bed. Her face and body had been painted with white enamel paint. She was moaning. He rushed to her and tried to soothe her.

'They rush in and hold me and do it to me one after the other,' she groaned. 'They call you Snowflake, and they say me Snowflake whore, so they paint me like snowflake and laugh at me.'

'I'll get the police. I'll get an ambulance.'

'No police, no ambulance – get Sammy!'

Sammy and his wife and many of the neighbours came without question. Sammy's wife got hot water, soap and towels and began to bathe Pocahontas. Sammy poured rum. The others brought buckets of water and started to clean the house. Somebody brought spare rolls of wallpaper.

'Who was da man what lead 'em?' asked Sammy.

'Leo the Lion,' wept Pocahontas.

'I'll get the police,' shouted Thomas.

'Ain't no need for that, mon,' said Sammy. 'We gotta see to ourselves in Moss Side.' He clicked his fingers. 'Hit him in da balls with lump of iron, poor damn Leo no longer a lion. Drink up da rum, mon, suit you fine. Me and da others make house shine.'

Pocahontas went to sleep, and Thomas crept downstairs. Everybody was hard at work. Already rolls of wallpaper were being pasted on the walls. His desk had been cleaned and polished, and there was a jam jar of artificial flowers on it. The house reeked with perfume and disinfectant. He swigged the rum.

175

It was mid-morning when he awoke. The house looked better than it did when his mother was alive, although the unmatched rolls of wallpaper were eye-catching: half a red rose came next to a yellow stripe. Sammy fried bacon and eggs.

'Everything honky-dory now, eh? Sun shine. Nice day. She gone.'

'Gone?'

Sammy snapped his fingers. 'Jamaican girl she up and go. She say get lost where de trade wind blow.'

Thomas watched his gods being brought out of the Hall. They were dropped on the steps, and a man with a two-handed mallet thudded them into powder; a boy swept up the powder and put it in a midden.

'Must you do that?' he asked the man with the mallet.

'Best talk to the gaffer,' said the man.

The gaffer came up to him; he had the unmistakable bog-trot of a lively Irishman; there was a bowler hat at an angle on his head; he carried a shillelagh to point things out with; he had an accent like Dick Wilson's; it could have been Dick talking.

'Well now, sir, in answer to your very endearing question, and 'tis pulverising 'em into powder so's they can't be vandalised, and that's a fact so it is.'

'But you are vandalising them.'

'Ah, no, sir.'

'They're gods and goddesses.'

'Is that true now?' He pointed to Venus, who was about to be turned into powder. 'Sure no self-respecting goddess would be showing her tits like Tilly Flop, would they now? And can ye imagine, me learned friend, how they'd be vandalising this fine young lady if she was to be dumped on the tip as she stands, for isn't that where all this stuff's going? On the tip at Barney's Field. Ach, and sure if she's a feminine god, like ye say, and like I'm not disputing, wouldn't them moochers and scavengers up on the tip be dedicating her, and no mistake?'

'The glory that was Greece ends up in a dustbin,' said Thomas.

'Ah, well, doesn't it come to us all? Is it not ashes to ashes, me wise man?' The gaffer looked down at Venus, and removed his bowler hat with reverence. 'A goddess did ye say?'

There was a loud crack and rumble. The mighty demolition ball had swung against the side of Ancoats Hall and sent it tumbling into a rising cloud of dust.

A lot of Ancoats had already gone. Thomas could actually see his school standing on its own in the middle of a waste land. Smoke from a dozen rubbish fires puffed up among the bricks. The largest fire was the heap of forms, staging and scenery of his children's theatre. He cycled across the waste land to his school.

It was the last day of Raglan Street School. About sixty pupils attended; they'd not been removed to the estates yet. There was a funeral atmosphere.

'Are you glad to be leaving Raglan Street and Ancoats?' he asked them.

'Yes and no,' was the general shout.

'Why no?'

'Because Ancoats is ours,' said O'Reilly. 'It belongs to us and no other kid in the world would dare to challenge us. But when we get to where we're going, we'll be called the kids from Shit Creek like we've always been called.'

'Then don't say you're from Ancoats.'

'They'll find out. They always do.'

'So you've no pride in Ancoats?'

'Please, sir, who the bloody hell could have pride in coming from Ancoats?' said Pieroni.

Thomas looked out through the window. Ancoats Hall was being destroyed; he needed some place to take them. Over and beyond Pollard Street the big empty mills were still standing. He marched them out of the class and into the shadows of these dead buildings; the shadows were blue; it was quiet apart from the occasional fluttering of a pigeon. He found a large stretch of waste ground surrounded by the buildings; this was where he was going to hold his last class.

'So you've no pride in Ancoats?'

'No, sir.'

'Well, let me tell you something. Right here where we're standing was once a very important shipbuilding yard; here among these dark satanic mills.'

There were sneers of 'Gerroff' and 'Pull the other leg, sir.' His class laughed.

'Very well, if you don't believe me, or if people you tell don't believe you, it can all be looked up in back editions of the *Manchester Guardian*. This was a shipbuilding yard, in the middle of the mills, and nowhere near the sea. It was started in 1830, when

178

a Scottish millwright took over a factory to make waterwheels; his name was William Fairbairn. He decided to build ships. Those were the days of wooden sailing ships, hearts of oak and that; but he built ironclads, some of the finest ironclads in the world; in fact, right where you're standing was built one of the first iron ships for the Royal Navy, the *Magaera*, and when it went into action it had an iron disc on its bridge which said "Made in Ancoats". Then they built the *Lord Dundas*, and do you know where it sailed? It was built for service on the Forth and Clyde Canal, and it sailed right down the Clyde, cocking a snook at the world's most famous shipbuilding river, and its disc said "Made in Ancoats".'

'How did they get 'em to the sea, sir?'

'I'm coming to that, for remember there was no Ship Canal; that wasn't built until sixty years later. One of their largest iron ships was the *Manchester*, it was a first-class vessel and there was no question of changing the name to anything silly like *Lancaster*. *Manchester* it was, and it had a capacity to carry fifty tons of cargo. The only place to launch it was in the River Irwell at Quay Street. It was kept in its scaffolding and put on wheels, and it was pulled by fourteen cart-horses; it took two days to lug the ship the two miles from here to the Irwell. It was as great a feat as anything in Homer's *Odyssey*. And what did it say on the disc?'

'Made in Ancoats!' shouted the class. Thomas knew he was in command; the class was his.

'Well, orders for Ancoats ships poured in, and one which would have made old Homer nod with approval was the *Vulcan*. It was ninety-eight feet long with a displacement of a hundred and eight tons, and it was ordered by a Zurich cotton merchant to carry his cotton on Lake Zurich, and that's in Switzerland, and Switzerland is surrounded by mountains and has no sea. So they built the ship – yes, right here – and then when they found it was watertight and could stand up to our Manchester rain, they dismantled it and took it plate by plate across the Pennines by cart-horse again. It was re-assembled at Selby in Yorkshire, sailed down the Humber all the way to Hull, crossed the gales of the North sea, and ploughed its way up the Rhine. It could go no further than the waterfalls at a place called Schaffhausen, then it was taken apart again and hauled by cart-horse across forty miles of tough countryside.'

179

Thomas gave a smirk, which announced he was going to tell something funny.

'It was named the *Vulcan* here in Ancoats. Now Vulcan was the Roman god of fire, probably copied from the Greek Hephaestus, and certainly a full-blooded male. But when it was launched on Lake Zurich, it was renamed *Minerva*. Now Minerva was a Roman goddess, probably copied from the Greek Pallas Athena, and very definitely every inch a lady. Perhaps some important little piece must have gone astray during all the dismantling.' There was a general giggle from the class. 'But *Vulcan* or *Minerva*, the ship made in Ancoats, was taken over the mountains to Switzerland. So you see, there's nothing to be ashamed of with the "Made in Ancoats" label. You lot can do whatever you set out to do, like Odysseus, and overcome all obstacles. Nothing is impossible.'

'Please, sir, will you take us to Louis Rocca's ice cream parlour now the lesson's over?'

'Certainly not,' said Thomas.

'But you just said nothing was impossible if you come from Ancoats.'

His last lesson cost Thomas two pounds, ten shillings.


Thomas cycled up the road as he had done for nearly forty years. He felt it was his bounden duty to stay with the school while it was being destroyed. With all the surrounding buildings and mills gone, he noticed for the first time that it was a beautiful building; it had lines and curves which he'd never before seen. He wore his frayed old tweed jacket, for he knew the dust would fly. The workmen all carried loud transistor radios.

Penny Lane is in my ears and in my eyes,
    There beneath the blue suburban skies
I sit and dream. Meanwhile back in Penny Lane
    There is a fireman with an hour glass.

Some men stood on the roof and flung slates down; others took great sledge-hammers to the ornamental stonework. The giant iron ball began swaying and cracking the walls to pieces. Everything tumbled, and the dust billowed. A mechanical grab

180

lifted slices of the walls and clattered them on trucks. A mechanical shovel followed behind scooping up the dust and smaller debris. The dust made him cough; his face became as grimy as the workmen's. Windows and blackboards cracked.

Yesterday, all my troubles seemed so far away,
   Now it looks as though they're here to stay,
Oh, I believe in yesterday.

An expensive car drove up, and a well-fed middle-aged gentleman nodded to his driver to wait. He lit a cigar and walked up to Thomas.

'Mr Davies, sir?'

'That's me.'

'I don't suppose you remember me? It's the glass eye; it fools everybody.'

'No, Keenan, I don't know who you are.'

'Bloody hell! You can't go wrong with names, can you, sir?'

'It used to be my job. Well, how are you?'

'Never better, sir. All this is mine.' He indicated the workmen and their contraptions. 'Y'see, having only one eye – I lost the other on park railings – I was no good for the forces, so I took me chance and went into demolition; finishing off what Hitler only half did.' He puffed on his cigar. 'One of the biggest contractors in the city, that's all. Never thought I'd be knocking me old school down though. Wasn't a bad school, was it, sir?'

'The finest school in town,' said Thomas.

'Have a cigar, sir.'

Thomas took the cigar and put it in his top pocket for later. 'I'd like a souvenir of the school, Keenan.'

'Best be quick then. Nowt much left.'

Thomas rooted around the rubble for something to take as a reminder. The only piece of anything intact was a lavatory seat. He pushed his arm through it and slung it over his shoulder.

Yesterday, love was such an easy game to play,
   Now I need a place to hide away,
Oh, I believe in yesterday.

He cycled away from all the smashing and crushing and tran-

181

sistor music, and for the first time in twenty years he took the old route back to Moss Side. The phrenology shop had been knocked down, but the College Arms was still there, and it seemed a good place in which to smoke a cigar. It had been a long time since he and Hopkins and Hayward had supped there as students. He went into the room where there would be students babbling their ignorance about Nietzsche, Hemingway, Aristotle, Scott Fitzgerald, Isis, Osiris, Ben Jonson and Marlowe. The man behind the bar stopped him, and tapped the lavatory seat.

'Workmen, sir, are asked to use the vault; that's the other room. Mostly the university crowd come in here and they'd make you feel out of place. By the way, seeing as you're in the lavatory business so to speak, I wonder if you'd mind having a look at the men's toilet before you go; it's bloody blocked. Worth a pint, eh?'

Thomas went into the vault; the window looked straight across Oxford Road to the Owens Collegs archway. He nodded hello to the archway as he sat down, sipped his pint of beer and lit his cigar.

What had happened since he'd last walked under that archway? He'd turned out tram drivers, tram guards, railway clerks, shipping clerks, warehousemen, packers, shop assistants, newspapermen, stage hands, laboratory technicians and on and on and on. And in between all that, he'd created a thousand or more navigators, a hundred or more radio operators, and for two air forces. He'd also turned out a pilot for a rival one. He had been loved by three beautiful girls of different religions and different hues. They'd always remain young and beautiful because he'd never see them again. He'd build a cottage in his brain and fill it with sink-deep-down comfortable furniture so that these girls could visit his brain any time they wished. And somewhere he had a son, a very clever son. What more could any man expect out of life? And the archway had been the archway to all that.

Thomas finished his pint, then went into the lavatory to see what he could do about the blockage. He made a plunger out of a mop, and plunged and plunged. An accumulation of excreta burst up from the bowl and covered his shoes and trouser bottoms. He stunk to high heaven, but he cleared the blockage.

'Right,' he said to the barman. 'Free pint, please!'

'Not in here, mate. Not stinking like that.' The barman gave him ten shillings. 'Here, go and buy it in the pub down the road; it'll send some of their custom up here.'

The private school was in Shropshire. It was a Tudor building with just enough ivy to make it like Thomas's imagined Grey-friars. It stood in beautifully kept grounds, with rhododendron bushes in bloom sedately placed. The stately school faced the Wrekin and the site of the Roman encampment of Uriconium. There was a rugby field and a cricket pitch. At the boundary of the school grounds was a small thatched cottage. Behind it, fields, hedges and trees sloped up to the Wrekin.

Thomas drove along the driveway in his little yellow Austin Seven, which he'd bought from Jack on condition it was sprayed yellow. He had a reference in his pocket from the Education Committee which merely stated he had been employed by them for forty years and had been honest, punctual and hard-working. He'd specifically asked the education office not to mention his having been a teacher.

'You seem ideal for the job,' said the headmaster, reading the reference. 'I advertised for a caretaker, preferably a retired wido-wer, for a small but important private school, and you seem to fill the bill. Sixty is young for retirement, and you look fit; I'm sure you've many years left. All we require from you is that you keep the classrooms and common room neat and tidy, clean the black-boards down every evening, make sure there's always chalk avail-able, and any other odds and ends. Well, you know the job I'm sure. Your flat is above the stable; it's only a small one, which is why we asked for a man on his own. Now, if you can find the kit-chen, Mrs Harrison will find you something to eat after your long drive.'

Emily Harrison was about the same age as Thomas; she was a widow; her husband had been headmaster of the school. When he died, they'd asked her to stay on as matron and cook, and they allowed her to live in the cottage on the boundary.

She was a happy woman, and a good-looking woman; she had a good figure; her hair, though white, was elegantly styled; she

184

looked like a charming duchess, and she talked like one. Her tiled kitchen contained a lingering smell of ground coffee beans; her coffee was so delicious that Thomas swirled it around his mouth before swallowing it. The tea she poured from her ornate teapot was equally delightful, and she could talk about various brands of tea as knowingly as he could discuss the different brands of pipe tobacco. He was always made welcome in her kitchen.

His job as caretaker was hardly a job. He merely wandered around corridors. He could sit on tall Elizabethan chairs outside classroom doors and listen to the lessons; sometimes he would nod up and down in agreement with what the master was saying; other times he would nod sideways with disagreement. He took messages and did errands for everybody.

A few weeks after he'd started, he went in to a classroom to clean the blackboard down. There was a chalked instruction – 'please leave.' The master had started a few sentences from Caesar's *Conquest of Britain* by putting it into Latin from an English translation lying on his desk. Thomas saw it as a challenge. He rubbed off the 'please leave' and proceeded to complete the blackboard with the Latin in his very best printing.

'Goodness gracious! Have you heard?' Emily asked him as she poured out two cups of tea. 'The boys are saying we've got a ghost. One of the Romans from across the fields at Uriconium. And I'm half sure the masters believe it too. It seems that during the night Mr Hunt's blackboard was filled with Latin, and perfect Latin at that. Thieves? Well, no, a thief would hardly break into a school to write Latin on the board, would he? I heard the headmaster say it wasn't a matter for the police.'

'I'm glad of that.'

'It's apparently from Julius Caesar's invasion of Britain, and with the Roman soldiers at Uriconium having taken part in it, well, you can imagine how the boys' minds are working. And it can't have been one of the masters playing a prank, because none of them know Latin well enough. I overheard Mr Hunt telling the headmaster he'd have to brush up on his Latin and the classics otherwise he'd have the ghost making a fool of him.'

'Then perhaps there'll be a few more passes to Oxford and Cambridge,' smiled Thomas.

'It's all right you joking, Thomas, but it's a mystery and no

185

mistake. I hope no Romans come knocking at my cottage door during the night. It was bad enough when we used to be afraid of German paratroopers.'

Thomas burst out laughing. 'Then 'twas the Roman, now 'tis I,' he bubbled.

'What's that? I've heard it somewhere.'

'Housman's poem about the Wrekin out there. "Then 'twas before my time, the Roman at yonder heaving hill would stare." '

'Shut up. I'll be dreaming.'

' "The gale, it plies the saplings double, it blows so hard, 'twill soon be gone. Today the Roman and his trouble are ashes under Uricon." And so are mine, Emily, so are mine.'

He was forced to tell her he was the ghost, and of course he had to tell her his profession.

'Why don't you tell the head you were a teacher?'

'And get fired? No, thank you. I like it here. This is *The Gem* and *The Magnet*. Don't breathe a word; just let the ghost walk.'

'But it could be helpful. Suppose a master were to be off ill or something?'

'Can you imagine the pupils writing home to tell their parents the Latin master had been ill, so they were taught by the care-taker? They'd take their kids away. Emily, I like it here; it's all I know; I've been around classrooms for fifty-five years, since I was five.'

'But such a waste!'

'Emily, those kids don't need anybody like me. They write with gold fountain pens. They'll end up as cabinet ministers and archbishops. I'm a bus drivers' teacher.'

Thomas's coach house was small. There was only one round window high up, and he had to stand on his desk to look out. His desk was one of the few things he brought with him; that and his bicycle and books. He'd burned all his mother's books in the back yard before he left Moss Side. It had been difficult fighting the temptation to flick through them, but he didn't want to find any more letters which had been used as bookmarks between the pages of moonlight enchantment, and he didn't want anybody else to find them; it was finished; the less he knew the better.

He began to take an interest in trees and shrubs; he hadn't seen many of them in his life; the countryside was all new to him;

it was his instinct to learn all he could about them. He sketched the trees, and painted them, and read up on their mythology. He talked to the trees. He could not only tell them why the gods had made them and who and what they really were, but advised them on what jobs to take up after they'd been felled, a wardrobe or a walking stick, a bench or a beam.

Emily went for walks through the coppice with him, and listened when he gave the trees lessons about themselves.

'You've got a vivid imagination, Thomas.'

'Life is imagination and nothing else,' he replied.

'Cuckoo! Cuckoo!' It was unmistakable; it filled the sky. They rushed to the edge of the coppice, and Thomas saw a solitary bird flapping in a straight line low over the meadows. 'Cuckoo! Cuckoo!'

'I've never seen a cuckoo before,' he told Emily.

'Not many have; it throws its voice. But that's a cuckoo, Thomas, and it means summer's coming. Pity they lay their eggs in other birds' nests.'


Thomas and Emily got married because of the school's need for a chemistry laboratory. Emily was informed that her cottage would have to be sold to help pay for it.

'We can't stand in the way of science,' said Thomas. 'Marry me and we'll buy the cottage. I've not touched my gratuities since the war; they've accumulated interest. I sold the old house in Moss Side, and I've got a pension and a wage, so who's complaining?'

There was comfort and security in their relationship. They argued together and laughed together. They enjoyed the same things, the same walks, the same weather, the same food. Thomas began to enjoy green salads, something he didn't remember having had before in his life. Her cottage had a constant smell of lavender and pipe tobacco; it shone with brasses. In a corner was a stately grandfather clock; it had been made in Shrewsbury two hundred years ago and still swung a slow steady pendulum to keep perfect time. She grumbled about him wanting to hang his lavatory seat, until he put a mirror behind it and hung it in the bathroom for shaving. He kept his old watch on the mantelpiece, always winding it before going to bed. The watch

187

lost five minutes every day; only once in a blue moon, and then for a short period, was it at the same time as the grandfather clock, but Thomas never adjusted it. On occasions when he mentioned his mother, she said: 'She seemed a very nice lady.'

There were afternoons when he got on his bicycle, which he'd painted yellow for fun, and cycled off down the lanes. Emily had an instinct never to ask where he was going.

He cycled to a narrow lane and walked across the meadows to the River Severn, where he sat motionless under an oak tree. There was never anybody waiting for him; he was never joined by anybody. Sometimes he saw a salmon riding the current, and it enthralled him until it swam away.

He returned home as though in a trance, usually lighting his pipe and staring at the old watch. There was no need for any instinct to tell Emily not to disturb him; she was far too busy cleaning the cow muck off his shoes, and off the carpets where he'd trodden it in.

A week before Christmas, a keen wind carried the boys' singing of 'In Dulce Jubilo' from the chapel across the playing fields to the cottage. Thomas sat at his desk and listened.

'Thomas.'

'Yes.'

'I've something to ask you. You can always say no.'

'Ask me.'

'The Women's Institute have asked me to ask you if you would give them talks. About trees.'

'Emily, they're countrywomen. They know all about trees.'

'For kindling, and for making home-made wine, yes. But they don't know the things about them, some of the naughty things, that you know. They meet in the old village schoolroom, and there's a blackboard.'

'I'll think about it.'

She knew that meant yes.

He picked up a sprig of mistletoe lying on his desk.

'According to Robert Graves in *The White Goddess*,' he said, 'the remains of mistletoe were found in a Bronze Age coffin at Gristhorpe near Scarborough. He criticises Frazer's *Golden Bough* for not making it clear that the druids cut the mistletoe from oak boughs as a phallic ritual. Mistletoe was supposed – '

'Oh, give it to me,' said Emily, snatching the mistletoe from him.

She kissed him under the mistletoe.